KU-509-077

MAGNUS FIN
AND THE
OCEAN QUEST

MAGNUS FIN
AND THE OCEAN QUEST

JANIS MACKAY

To Megan
+ Orla
♡

Janis Mackay

Kelpies

Kelpies is an imprint of Floris Books

First published in 2009 by Floris Books
Second printing 2010

© 2009 Janis Mackay

Janis Mackay has asserted her right under the
Copyright, Designs and Patents Act 1988
to be identified as the Author of this Work.

All rights reserved. No part of this book may
be reproduced without the prior permission of
Floris Books, 15 Harrison Gardens, Edinburgh
www.florisbooks.co.uk

The publisher acknowledges a Lottery grant
from the Scottish Arts Council towards the
publication of this series.

British Library CIP Data available

ISBN 978-086315-702-8

Printed in Poland

For Eirinn and Saul

Chapter One

Hello whoever you are,
My name is Magnus Fin.
I'm glad you picked me out of the sea. In three weeks
I am eleven. I've got a Neptune's Cave in my room, with
bottles and bits of boats and shells and funny shaped wood
and treasure off sunken ships. I live beside the sea. If
anybody finds this I want to have a best friend, and I
want to be more brave. I want my parents to be happy
like they used to be. I hope eleven is good. Maybe we will
meet. Whoever finds this — we can be best friends. I have
different eyes, one green and one brown, but I am fine and
like I said my name is Magnus Fin.
Good luck

Magnus Fin rolled up the small sheet of paper
and fed it carefully down through the bottle
neck then corked the dark green glass bottle. It
was ten o'clock at night but this far north come
midsummer it hardly got dark. He ran down to
the shore then leapt easily over the craggy rocks.
When he was as far out as he could go he swung
his arm once, twice, three times, then flung the old
green glass bottle out to sea.

The water was smooth. The bottle hit the
surface with a plop, vanished for a moment, then

floated back up to the surface where the out-going tide carried it away.

Magnus Fin watched until his bottle was a tiny speck, bobbing in the distance. "Good luck," he shouted after it, then turned and jumped from rock to rock until he was back on the sand.

Once more he turned and peered out to sea. His bottle had gone. With excitement pounding in his chest he ran back home along the shore.

"Where were you, Magnus?" his mother called from her darkened bedroom. Her voice sounded thin and wispy. Magnus Fin gently closed the front door of their small cottage and stood in the half-light of the living room.

"Just down at the sea," he said, still panting from his run. "It's still light."

"And late, laddie. What else are they going to say about us, with you running about like an urchin? Come through here and let me see you for a second." His mother's words sounded dry and anxious coming from her darkened room. Magnus Fin, biting his nails, breathed deeply then took his ragged nail out of his mouth and stepped into his parents' bedroom to say good night.

"It's still so light, Mum. Sun's still up," he said, peering through the dim light to where he could just make out the hunched figure of his mother sitting up in bed. Red rays from the setting sun stole through a slit in the closed curtains and fell upon his mother's ancient-looking face. Though he had looked upon his mother like this for some years now, and often in darkened rooms, it still shocked him to see how withered and lined she had become.

"I threw a message in a bottle out to sea," he said, "that's all."

"Oh, did you, son? What for?"

"For fun. And – and I made a wish."

"Good, Magnus. That's good. We could do with wishes. Were there any waves to speak of?" his mother asked, her words slow and shaky.

"No. Sea's still flat as a pancake," he said, edging backwards. He wanted to be gone from this dark, sad place. He wanted to be in his own room, which he'd made into a treasure trove full of the findings he'd combed from the beach. And he didn't want to tell his mother about his wishes. If he told her they might not come true. Everybody knew that.

"Anyone out and about?" she asked.

"No. Not down at the beach, but I could hear music. I think there's a dance on in the village hall, Mum. I heard the band playing. You should go sometimes, you and Dad. You can still walk. You could dance; Granny told me you were a great dancer. You still could, so could Dad," Magnus Fin said, hurt choking his voice. "You could. I don't know why you won't. You could ..."

His mother shook her white-haired head from side to side.

"Wheesht, son. We're better here, better staying quiet. Run off to bed now. Your dad will come through soon to say good night. Go on, laddie, off with you."

She gave a slow wave of her hand, and Magnus Fin, muttering good night, went through to his bedroom. He wished for the millionth time that his parents *did* go to the ceilidh every Friday night in

the village hall, *and* the pub, *and* the badminton
and did all the other things normal parents did.

In the quiet of his room Magnus Fin picked
up the rusty bell he had found on the shore that
morning. His treasures made everything better.
The old bell felt heavy in his young hand. He
gazed at the round rusty thing. At least it could
have been a bell on a ship once, he thought, or
very much hoped. A big sailing ship – or a cruise
liner even – like the fancy ships he'd seen passing
on their way to Orkney. He lifted it up and felt the
weight of the iron. Even the bell that might have
tolled on the ill-fated *Titanic* couldn't ring away his
gloomy mood. And the feeling of gloom, he knew,
was because of the cruel words he'd overheard in
the village that afternoon about his parents.

"Och, them?" a man had said in the shop,
shaking his head, not seeing the boy behind him.
"Something right funny about them!"

And Magnus Fin, though he wanted to stand
up for his parents, didn't have the courage to
say anything. Instead he ran out of the shop,
forgetting all about the comic and the fudge he had
wanted to buy.

Now, in the peace of his own room, a hundred
thoughts ran through his head. *Something right
funny about them!*

Thing is, the man in the shop was right. There
was something funny about them *and* their son,
and not in a ha-ha way either. And the older
Magnus Fin got, the more he noticed something
was wrong. Magnus Fin had, as he wrote in his
message in a bottle, uncanny eyes: one green, one

brown. And as if that wasn't uncanny enough, his pupils were not black but dark blue. And there was something else wrong with him, though he made sure no one ever saw. His feet were webbed, just slightly, between the toes.

And to top all that, his parents had a terrible affliction. They were *strange*! They weren't hippies or Goths, geeks or organic gardeners, motorbike riders or train spotters, jail-birds or communists. No – they were much stranger than that! Ragnor and Barbara, Magnus Fin's parents, looked ancient. I don't mean fifty with a few grey hairs, laughter lines and double chins. No – I mean, though Magnus Fin was only ten years old, his parents looked nigh on one hundred. And what unsettled the village folk was that Ragnor and Barbara, only years before, had been young, fit and handsome. Then suddenly they had seemed to age and fade beyond their years.

Some of the villagers, thinking the aging affliction might be catching, kept well away. Of course a few friendly souls in the village came calling with catalogues or raffle tickets or toys for the boy, but even they stopped calling when Barbara refused to answer the door.

So Magnus Fin had a fairly lonely life. He was the butt of most of the jokes at school and usually stood by himself at playtime, reading a book, flicking his marbles across the ground or staring into space. He wished he was brave enough to join in the other children's games, or stick up for his parents, but the thought of standing up to the kids who teased him the most made his knees quake.

So at school he stood on his own, him and his strange eyes staring into space. At least the other pupils thought the "weirdo" Magnus Fin was staring into space. They didn't know he was off at sea, under the waves, or surfing, or diving, or picking velvet crabs out of rock pools, or finding treasure from sunken ships. And when the rude man in the shop had said that very afternoon, with a sneer in his voice, "Och, them? Something right funny about them!" Magnus Fin could only bite his lip, turn on his heels and run.

Now, holding the rusty bell, he tried not to think about all of that. He heard his mother softly sobbing in the room next door, like she did most nights. He got up and went to his window. A huge moon rose over the water. Unlike his parents he never closed his curtains. He lifted the piece of rusty iron and held it up then swung it back and forth, imagining it ringing out to warn all aboard a storm was coming.

He heard his father shuffling about in the living room. Ragnor would come through soon to wish his son good night. Sleep, though, felt a long way off for Magnus Fin. Perhaps it was the light of midsummer plus the effect of the full moon, but Magnus Fin's head was in a spin. Snatches of gossip churned around his mind, harsh words he'd overheard in the village. They all came back now, squawking like crows inside his head:

"Thon old couple down at the shore, their problem is they don't eat meat, that's what's wrong with them!" That was Mrs Gow, the butcher's wife. "Aye, mark my words – no meat, no looks."

"Ach! I heard they overdid the sunbathing and that's when they started to look a hundred." That was pasty-faced Mrs Gunn, who was a great believer in factor fifty sunscreen. "I don't trust the ozone myself," she had added, folding her white arms and frowning.

"Naw, naw. That's no the real reason. The real reason is they went off to California to have face lifts and look what happened!" said wee Patsy Mackay. Magnus Fin saw her now in his mind's eye, gasping and holding her face together as though the aging might all of a sudden come upon her and her face might drop off.

He imagined all the gossips huddled together in a sinking ship, screaming as salt water came over them and his old bell rang out their death knell.

Then he thought that was probably a bit unkind – after all, "Words don't hurt," as his father was forever saying. So Magnus imagined them all bundled together in a ship, getting a good old soaking instead.

It was late now, and dark. Magnus Fin's eyelids grew droopy. He put his bell on a shelf next to his starfish then climbed into bed. His bed was a boat in which he set sail into an underwater dreamland each night. Whatever names he'd been called during the day – Alien Eyes or Walking Stick or Chicken Heart or Face Mistake – never seemed to matter as much when he was in his bed drifting off to sleep. Sleep made everything all right again. And dreams.

Before Magnus fell asleep that night his dad came in to say good night, like he always did.

Ragnor lifted his son's hands and saw that the nails were bitten down to the skin. The man with the long grey hair and leathery, lined face stroked his son's dark hair and whispered kindly, "Try not to worry, lad; this is how we are now."

"But I get called names, Dad. I don't like it."

"You know what they say about sticks and stones breaking your bones and names not hurting you?"

"Well, it's not true," said Magnus Fin, "and I am scared of them." But his voice was drowsy now. His father's words drifted into his half-sleep as though they were coming from a long way off.

"It could be worse," Ragnor continued, stroking his son's hand. "Folks will talk and call you names. Some folk are just like that. They don't know better. Dinny heed them, Fin. Be proud of who you are. It's no bad thing to be different. You're special, my lad; if only you knew just how special you are. For now, just get on with life as best you can. Good night, Fin."

As Ragnor left the room he muttered something about the sea and it giving Fin courage ... but by that time Magnus Fin was sound asleep.

Chapter Two

For Magnus Fin, getting on with life as best he could meant going down to the seashore, splashing about in the cold North Sea, diving with his mask and snorkel and beach-combing for the treasures the tide brought in. With water he was brave. With water he was happy. It was in standing up to other people that his knees went wobbly. But for most of the time – after school, weekends and holidays – there were no other people, not children to play with anyway.

Often he played alone in his bedroom, his "Neptune's Cave". He had decorated it with his fantastic findings, so when he wasn't at school he was likely to be in one of two places: at the beach or in his room. Hanging from his bedroom ceiling was an old brown fishing net with yellow corks. On his shelves made from driftwood he'd placed clam shells and Chinamen-hat shells, patterned stones, coloured glass and bones. In a wooden box under his bed he kept his extra special treasure – weird and wonderful bits from the wrecks in the Pentland Firth or the *Titanic*, the Spanish Armada or pirate ships.

In this treasure box he had a metal sign that said GENTLEMEN and another that said UPPER DECK.

Magnus Fin was sure that these faded metal signs had once adorned the great ships of old. He had hundreds of bits of broken plates in another box that had, he was certain, once been dinner plates on the great ship the *Titanic*. Now the plates, all broken, were like a jigsaw. Magnus Fin would spread out the pieces on his bedroom floor and try to make a plate. When he had something that vaguely resembled a round shape he would put a biscuit on the patchwork plate and pretend he was dining on the *Titanic*. Then, when the ship struck an iceberg and started to sink, it would be Magnus Fin who ran about rescuing everyone – but he had to do it quietly because he didn't want to wake his parents. Then he'd be hailed a hero and have his picture on the front page of the local newspaper and everyone at school would want his autograph. Magnus Fin loved his treasures from the beach.

It was his mother who first named her son's room Neptune's Cave. "But I'm not fit enough now to clean it for you, son. Cleaning's too much effort – you'll have to do that yourself," she said one day as she hobbled through the house puffing and panting.

"That's no bother to me, Mum," he said, grinning and waving a duster in the air, "I'll definitely keep it spic and span." It was his private room full of his private treasures.

She nodded her old white head and shuffled off across the hallway. Barbara spent most of her days in the kitchen listening to the radio while making soup or gutting the fish her husband managed to catch. Her evenings and nights she spent reading books or watching television in bed. Cleaning was something that happened less and less in the cottage down by the sea.

Magnus Fin's grandmother visited every Sunday, but as a rule Barbara didn't like these visits – not when her mother looked much, much younger than herself, and insisted on tidying up and rearranging the kitchen, and sighing and saying the place was a blooming mess. But Magnus looked forward to these visits because with Granny May on a Sunday afternoon there was always some laughing, singing and storytelling about the house. She might be a "wee busy-body", as Barbara called her, but she brought life and shine to the little cottage by the shore.

It was Sunday, and because it was rainy Magnus Fin was in his room playing with his pirate ship. Granny popped her head round the door and asked if she could just peep at her grandson's treasures. "I promise I won't disturb them," she said, "and I won't clean up either. Just a teeny wee peep, eh?" So Magnus Fin let her in to Neptune's Cave, and felt his chest swell up with pride when his grandmother whistled in wonder.

"What a grand place you have here, Fin – my goodness me, that bell looks like it once tolled the time on a tall sailing ship full of one-eyed pirates."

"You're right there, Granny May. And look, here's a sign from the *Titanic* – the gentlemen's toilet sign. Isn't it the best thing in the whole world?"

"Goodness mercy me – the very best in the universe. Just think – poor men – looking up at the sign as they went off innocently to the toilet, them never guessing it would be for the very last time. Oh, Fin, imagine all that salt water covering your face, filling your lungs – how awful." Granny May looked like she would burst into tears.

To change the subject, and move to another of his favourite topics, Magnus Fin sank down on to his bed, patting it for Granny to come and cuddle up next to him.

"Tell me what Mum was like before," he said. His mother had gone for her nap and his father had gone out fishing. Magnus always asked for that story – every Sunday – and Granny May always told it to him.

"Oh, all right, my boy. If I can just get comfy on this boat bed of yours then I'll tell you all about your beautiful mother."

He had to make sure his mother was out of hearing range. It was part of their game. Magnus Fin jumped up and closed his bedroom door.

"Ready lad? Coast clear?" she called.

"All clear, Captain," he said, saluting like a sailor. Then with a leap he jumped aboard and squashed up next to her on the bed.

"Well then, once upon a time Barbara, your mother, was the belle of the county. Lads used to come from as far as Inverness for the dances in our village, just in the hope she might partner them in a Gay Gordons or a Strip the Willow or one of these disco things. Oh, she had bonnie warm brown eyes and a sweet red mouth that

was forever smiling and her hair was a curtain
of coppery curls. And the pretty dresses she had!
Goodness, her wardrobe was bursting with them.
Cost me a fortune! But I didn't mind, Fin; she
looked such a picture in them. And high-heeled
shoes, and fancy jackets and dangly earrings.
She loved to dress up did your mother. Height of
fashion she was. And what a dancer! And did I tell
you about her singing?"

Magnus Fin nodded. Yes, he'd heard about
her singing and dancing and dressing up, but he
needed to hear about it again and again and again.
His grandmother ruffled his mop of black hair,
kissed him on the cheek and carried on.

"Oh, she had a voice I can tell you, like a
nightingale. And like you, my lad, she was forever
messing about down at the seashore. She could
have married a lord, so she could. Well, she married
your father and they were the happiest, bonniest
couple in the north. Strange wedding, mind you,
Magnus. Oh, it was great fun and the salmon on
the table was second to none, but your dad invited
none of his family. Not one! Which meant I had
to do most of the work. Well, they got this wee
cottage at the shore and everything was fine. Your
dad got a job up at the farm and people say he was
a good worker and your beautiful mother worked
in the jewellers in town. Well, you were born and
what a lovely wee boy you were. Then not long
after your third birthday something happened.
The good Lord knows what because I don't, but in
a jiffy all the beauty and youth in the pair of them
went away. You'd think someone had gathered it

up in a jug then poured it down the drain. Gone. *Puff!* Just like that."

Magnus Fin bit his bottom lip. He never enjoyed this part of the story.

"No one knows what happened," Granny May went on, shaking her head, "and if I've asked my daughter once, I've asked her a thousand times. But you just remember, boy, she was a beauty, and for that matter, so was your father. Now, lad, is there a cup of tea for your grandmother? Hm? All this speaking has made me as dry as a cork. And a wee biscuit too if you can spare it."

Magnus Fin jumped up, went through to the kitchen and made his grandmother tea. She had taught him to make tea, and toast and porridge. And she taught him to sing "You Cannae Shove Your Granny Off a Bus." He came back with the tea, singing away to himself.

"You are a great wee singer too. Just like your mother. And a little bird told me there's a boy having a birthday soon," she said, slurping her tea and winking at him over the rim of the cup. Magnus Fin nodded and grinned. "And what will that wee laddie who is going to be eleven be wanting?" she asked.

Magnus Fin shrugged his shoulders. What he really wanted was what he'd asked for in the glass bottle he'd thrown out to sea. Apart from those things he would like a bike, but he didn't know if his grandmother could afford a bike. Maybe it was too big a present to ask for. Usually she got him books and pencils and swimming trunks and jigsaws and sweeties. She lived in a little council house on her own in John O'Groat's. He didn't think she could afford a bike.

"A book about sharks would be good," he said. His grandmother looked relieved. "Well, if you're sure that's all you want I'll do my best," she said brightly, dunking her chocolate biscuit into her tea. "Now then, I'd better be getting back. Doing my line dancing tonight. Don't want to go missing that bus now, do I?"

Then Granny was off and the small cottage by the sea fell back into its quietness. Barbara lay sleeping. Ragnor was down by the shore. Magnus Fin went through to his room, carefully put away his *Titanic* treasures and counted the days to his birthday.

Chapter Three

The bonnie couple that Magnus's grandmother spoke of were now bent and grey and wrinkled. They were little more than thirty years old but looked at least a hundred! The days of dressing up and dancing seemed to have gone for ever. There was not a mirror in the house that his mother had not broken, and lately Barbara had taken to wrapping her face in a shawl so only her eyes could be seen. When she ate her soup at suppertime she brought a hand to her face, and when the postman or the catalogue lady came calling she took to her bed, so that no one should clap eyes on her. Often Barbara, so ashamed of her haggard appearance, cried herself to sleep. On those nights Magnus Fin held spiral shells up to his ears so that the drone of the sea would drown out his mother's crying. And the sea that came from his shells made a fine song, booming some nights and sighing others. Magnus Fin fell asleep to the slow hush of small waves lapping on the shore and woke to the same.

Come daybreak he was up and out. There was the sea otter to watch fishing for her breakfast of sea urchins at the shore. There were the seals to say good morning to – the kind-eyed creatures

with their noses rising out of the water seemed
to know just when Magnus Fin would be up and
about. And there was the tidemark to study, to
see what had been washed ashore overnight.
Sometimes, if his tummy was rumbling, he'd
pull limpets and winkles from the rock and suck
their juicy contents down in one suck. He loved
them.

He knew every stone, every rock. He knew where
the heron slept. He knew where the oystercatchers
raised their young. He knew the difference between
a shag and a cormorant. He knew where the
polecat prowled and saw every morning whether
a rabbit had been killed or not. He knew so much
but the pity was, he thought, he had no friend to
share it with.

On this morning he took up a flat stone and
skimmed it. The surface of the water was smooth.
The waves were baby waves, hardly worth jumping
over. His stone skimmed seven times. His record
was nine but seven was still good. His father, he
remembered, had taught him a verse: one for a
minnow, two for a cod, three for a reel and four for
a rod, five for a dolphin, six for a seal, seven for a
shark, so squeal baby squeal!

He laughed remembering the verse and the
tickling that always came at the end. His father
had been young then and full of life. It had been
a long while since he'd been tickled. Magnus
Fin scuffed at some stones. His job was to bring
home driftwood for the fire. On the stones he
found a thick plank. It could have come from a
broken hull. He dragged it along the beach and

back to his house. He might be thin but Magnus was strong.

His father was resting against the dry-stone wall by the cottage and calling to his son, "Good work, son – that's a fine bit of firewood. It's time for school. Don't be late! Find any treasure today?"

"Two dead rabbits and a cormorant's skull. But I left the rabbits," Magnus said, lowering the plank with one hand and with the other showing his dad the delicate shape of the white bird skull.

"She's a beauty," Ragnor said, nodding his old grey head and handing Magnus his school bag. "Now, go on, son – school!"

Magnus Fin placed the bird skull carefully in his bag and headed off in the direction of the village school. Somehow he couldn't run to school the way he could run to the beach. He dragged his heels and wished it was Saturday, Sunday or best of all, the summer holidays.

"Late again, Magnus Fin," said the teacher, Mrs McLeod, who was marking the register. She looked up when the strange wee boy closed the squeaky door of the classroom as quietly as he could. "What's the excuse this time?"

"Sorry," he said, his voice a tiny whisper, "slept in."

Mrs McLeod had almost given up hope with Magnus Fin. She had even gone so far as to buy him an alarm clock. But when her husband, a fisherman, told her that he regularly saw the boy at the beach at six in the morning, Mrs McLeod knew sleeping in was not the problem.

"Slept in where exactly?" she asked. The whole class now turned to stare at Magnus, who was trying without success to slip unnoticed on to his seat.

"Bed," he lied, his face turning red. Some of the children in his class giggled.

"Being late is bad enough," the teacher went on, "and telling lies is even worse. The cupboard needs tidying and you, Mr Magnus Fin, can do it. You can stay back after school today and help me. Right, class, let's get on. Now, P6 – what do you know about Mexico?"

Chapter Four

"So, Magnus Fin, what's so fascinating about the beach first thing in the morning?" the teacher asked that day after school when the other pupils had all gone home.

"It's always different, Miss," he said, handing Mrs McLeod a box full of jotters. This was his detention for being late, but the truth was he didn't mind staying on after school. "Like, um, the tide brings things in and I have to check," he went on, his voice excited now. "If I don't I might miss something great. My favourite is bits from sunken ships. And I got something today – wait a minute, Miss, and I'll show you – I've got a cormorant's skull."

Magnus left the teacher standing with her arms full of jotters and ran to his school bag and gently lifted out the cormorant's skull. "See! I've got loads of stuff and I sometimes help birds if they've got broken wings and I helped a baby seal that was stuck inside a washing basket."

"Goodness me! That's a good skull. Poor thing, but what on earth was a washing basket doing on the beach in the first place?"

"Dunno, Miss," he said, carefully placing the skull back in his bag. He returned to the cupboard, awaiting his next instruction.

"Pass me those crayons, will you? Good – and those paintbrushes. That wee Bobby Morrison has been putting his paintbrush away without cleaning it. Look! It's ruined. You'll have to throw it out. No wonder this school has no money. Oh, what a mess this cupboard is in. What is the world coming to? I don't know. Washing basket, what next?"

Mrs McLeod, tutting and sighing, took the dirty paintbrushes from Magnus Fin and dropped them in the bin, then struggled trying to lift the boxes of art equipment on to a shelf. With another sigh she turned to look at Magnus who was now busy stacking boxes of jotters in the cupboard. "Magnus Fin, you really should stick up for yourself you know. I heard that bully Sandy Alexander in the corridor. I heard what he called you – and your parents."

Magnus felt his face flush red. He stared at the floor. He'd heard Sandy Alexander too. "Decrepit lepers," he'd said. It sounded bad the way he had said it, though Magnus Fin didn't know what it meant. He just shrugged.

"And, um … how are your parents these days?"

"OK, I suppose. I mean, well, they seem … quite old and – and don't do much," Magnus Fin stammered, glad he was in the dark of the cupboard.

"Strange, isn't it? I mean, do doctors know what the problem is exactly? You know, the aging so fast thing." Mrs McLeod was stacking the artwork into a pile, not looking at Magnus Fin.

"My dad says we're all different and I just have to get on with life. There's a mousetrap here. Do you want it out?"

"Oh, no! Don't touch it," she shouted. "Anyway, I think we've done enough for one day. Yes, your dad is right of course. We are all different. Now that we're talking about being different, Magnus, I can't help wondering about your eyes – if you don't mind me asking. Do they run in your family? Have the doctors ever said anything about them?"

Magnus Fin imagined a line of doctors in white coats giving clever speeches about people. As far as he was aware no doctor had ever said anything. Magnus Fin had lied once already that day. He decided twice wouldn't make much difference.

"That I am special," he blurted out, feeling as soon as he'd said it that it wasn't a lie. He was special. "Can I go now, Miss?"

"Yes, yes. Off you go. And, Magnus – special or not – be on time on Monday, promise?"

Magnus Fin grinned at Mrs McLeod, nodded then sped off. His dad would be down at the beach looking for him, and his mother would be bringing her soup to the table, the soup she'd laboured over all day long. Running home he could almost smell it. He was starving.

Chapter Five

That night, after supper, and after swimming in the sea with his wetsuit on, and after making a fire on the beach and toasting half a packet of marshmallows, Magnus Fin fell into bed exhausted. As he was about to drift off to sleep he heard the sobs of his mother coming from the room next door and the low tones of his father's voice. Magnus pressed his ear to the wall and listened: "You should never have come ashore, Ragnor. Look at me, a decrepit hag. I'd be young still if it wasn't for you. I wish I had never set eyes on you!" Barbara cried.

There was that word again – *decrepit*. Magnus Fin usually held his hands over his ears through these arguments but tonight he wanted to hear more. Maybe it was something to do with turning eleven, but for once he really wanted to understand his parents and their strange illness.

"If it wasn't for your deed, woman, we would both be young," said Ragnor. "Now hush or you'll wake the lad." Magnus Fin had heard this before, this crying and blaming. Now he began to think, maybe whatever it was that was wrong with his parents was somehow his fault. His eyes *were* strange. He knew that. No one in school had eyes like his. And his grandmother had told him the illness began after his third birthday. What had he done? He loved his parents. He wanted them to be happy. But always this crying, blaming, moaning, wailing!

He had heard enough. He held shells up to his ears, hummed a tune along with the sound of the waves and eventually fell asleep, off to sea in his boat. He dreamt he was playing tig in the playground at school. Then he dreamt he was swimming under the sea and a beautiful girl was swimming by his side.

When he woke early next morning the sun was streaming in the window. He loved Saturdays. Quick as it takes to throw on a t-shirt and pair of shorts he was up and out. Thank goodness for the sea, for the shore, the sand, the rock pools, the treasures the tide brought in, the oystercatchers and screeching gulls and the lone heron that stood hunched over a rock, staring at the flat sea. Magnus Fin loved the sea and the shore. He forgot his troubles when he was by the sea.

It seemed to him that his father loved the sea too. Every day Ragnor walked slowly along the shore to a place where he cast his fishing line out to sea. Every evening there was fish on the table, herring or mackerel. Barbara gutted the fish and cooked it, humming away to whatever was crackling from her radio. There were times when even Barbara forgot her troubles and sang away to herself, the old pop songs she used to love. Then Ragnor would put a shaky hand around his wife's waist and kiss her lined face and the rare sound of laughter would light up the little cottage. Magnus Fin loved those times and wished this laughing and singing could go on for ever.

Ragnor, when he wasn't fishing, often sat in his cave by the sea. When Magnus was very young this had been the storytelling cave. He remembered the wonderful stories of life under the sea, and the way his father spoke brought the magical watery world to life. He would carry the boy on his back, striding out across the shore. And they'd make great sand castles and dig sand holes all the way to Australia. But though that was only a few short years ago, it may as well have been another lifetime.

Magnus Fin looked at his father now, limping slowly along the beach path with his grey head bent low and his thin legs shuffling shakily. What had happened? The other parents he saw every day standing at the school gates seemed much younger. Why did the clock in his house whirr so much faster?

Magnus Fin followed his father along the beach path to his cave. He ran to catch up, hoping for a story. After all, he was still a child, wasn't he? But his father sat in the cave in silence, staring out at the stillness of the sea. It seemed there were no more stories.

"When you are older, son," he said, looking slowly up at Magnus Fin, who stood expectantly at the mouth of the cave, "there will be other stories to tell you. Stories that will shock you to the core, but not now lad, you're too young." Ragnor's voice sounded weak and shaky.

"Please tell me now," pleaded Magnus, stepping inside the cave.

"It's not yet time, Fin," said Ragnor, his face as wrinkly as the furrowed waves. Then he was silent for a long while.

"Look, son," he suddenly said, pointing out to the sea. "Do you see how flat the sea is? Have you wondered where the big waves have gone?"

Magnus Fin turned to stare out at the great ocean in front of them. It *was* flat, crinkly with the brush of the breeze, but it was true, there were no waves. Now that Magnus thought about it, there had been no big waves for a very long time. He couldn't remember the last time he had watched mighty rollers crash against the rocks or got out his surfboard.

"It worries me," said Ragnor. "Something's not right in the world under the sea and there's nothing I can do about it. The waves clean the sea – and the waves have gone."

Magnus Fin sat silent, hunched on his stone. Out at sea screeching herring gulls circled over the flat water. His father stared at them, talking as though he had forgotten his son was with him.

"Aye, no waves is not good. The sea has fallen on bad times. These small teacup waves hardly bother to break on the stones. It'll be dirty in there, right dirty. Makes me think Neptune himself has fallen asleep. And all I can do is sit here and worry."

"Don't worry, Dad!"

Ragnor looked round, startled. "Ach! You gave me a fright, laddie. That's what happens when you get old, you haver away to yourself. Don't heed me, Fin."

"But you're not really old, are you?" the boy blurted out. "Why do you and Mum look so old?" Of course he had asked many times before but was never given an answer. Lately he had given up asking, but now it came again, out of his mouth before he could stop himself. "People at school say you must be ill, and Mum too. I've heard her crying at nights. The teacher said the doctors should know. Are you both ill? Are you?" Ragnor, staring now at his son, saw a tear glisten in his boy's eye in the red glow of the sun.

"Ill? Aye, in a way. That's all part of the story, son. Don't ask yet. When you're eleven. Then I'll tell you. I promise, Fin. We'll come back to the cave and we'll make a fire and I'll tell you the strangest story you ever heard. Until then, son, don't ask me."

Magnus nodded his head. His father spoke as though being eleven was a long way off. Had he forgotten? His only child would be eleven years old in two weeks time.

"That's soon, Dad," he said, thinking suddenly of the bottle he'd thrown out to sea. He wondered where it was now and whether anyone had found it.

His father nodded his stooping head. "Aye, Fin," he said in a hushed voice, "soon and not soon enough. At long last you'll be eleven – the age between the worlds. We'll come back here and you'll get your story. And you'll get more than you ever bargained for. You might be sorry you ever asked for a story then. Now let's get back, eh? Your mum might be worried, wondering where we've got to. Porridge will be cold."

They walked slowly back along the shore in silence, but it was all Magnus Fin could do to stop the excitement from jumping him up and down. He wanted to call out to the gulls, he wanted to shout to the sea, he wanted to hug his father. Some big change was on the way; he felt it in his bones. And it was something to do with turning eleven.

That very night, after his mother had cried herself to sleep, Magnus Fin picked up his prize starfish, turning it this way and that in the rays of the setting sun. The way the star flashed red lit up the boy's face. Something good was coming; he was sure of it.

Chapter Six

That Monday Tarkin arrived from America. The new boy in school, rather than being wary of Magnus Fin like everyone else, thought he had never seen such phenomenal eyes in his life.

"I am just so through with boring," said Tarkin, who dashed over to talk to Magnus Fin at break. "I've been round the world, I've lived with Inuits and Aborigines but man, no one, like, no one has eyes as way-out as yours. Can I be your friend? That would be so cool."

No one had ever asked Magnus Fin to be their friend before. He grinned. He recalled the way his starfish had glowed. He remembered the green bottle he had flung out to sea. He knew something good was coming. This was it – Tarkin!

Tarkin was tall with blond hair down past his shoulders, which he wore in a ponytail. He had two earrings hooped in his left earlobe and stick-on tattoos all up his arms. He wore a shark's tooth round his neck and kept a photograph of his first dog in his school bag. He took it out to show Magnus.

"Samson," said Tarkin sadly, "an Akita and the best friend ever. Got knocked down by a bus in New York. Gone now."

Magnus Fin touched Tarkin lightly on the shoulder. "I'm really sorry about that," he said, and for a moment the two boys stared down at the half-torn, thumbed photo of Samson. Then Tarkin put the photo carefully back in his school bag and cheered up.

"So what's it like here?" he asked, swinging his black rucksack on to his back and shaking his ponytail. "Like, is there anything to do around here?"

"Well, there's the beach," said Magnus Fin, "and there's the caves and I've got lots of treasures. Um, do you want to come and see?"

"Sure. You just said three of my all time favourite words – beach, cave and treasure. Wow! I can't wait!"

"Great – um, you could come after school if you want?"

"Sure, that'd be cool," said Tarkin.

Magnus felt his mouth stretch into a wide smile that almost hurt his face. He felt happy and sad. Happy because it seemed he had found a friend at last and sad because as soon as Tarkin saw his parents that would probably be the end of the friendship. He opened his mouth to try and explain but no words came, and he stood in the playground like a gaping fish.

"Hey, man, that's a great impersonation of a cod. Wanna see my shark impression?" Tarkin didn't wait for an answer. He pulled back his mouth to bare his teeth then started running after Magnus, singing the theme tune to *Jaws* as he did. Magnus Fin giggled then ran across the playground, pursued by a shark which jumped on him then pretended to eat him but tickled him instead. The two boys lay on the grass laughing and Magnus had never been happier in his life.

Tarkin sat beside Magnus Fin in school, and Magnus couldn't keep the smile off his face. This was the best birthday present ever – and he wasn't even eleven yet. He noticed Tarkin had a big wristwatch that he said could work underwater, and beside it he wore a beaded leather string wrapped several times around his wrist. While Mrs McLeod was talking, Tarkin drew a picture of a mermaid in his jotter.

"You bairns are the future generation and it's up to you to look after our planet – muckle great thing like a planet doesn't grow on trees." Tarkin brought out a pair of scissors from his rucksack, hiding them with his elbow from the teacher. He couldn't understand a word Mrs McLeod was saying.

"And as the future generation, you should know that all the herring have gone. So what are you going to do about it? Clean the beach, that's what! And what about the waves? Some morbid ones say the sea is dying!"

Tarkin cut out his drawing of the mermaid and pushed it across to Magnus Fin. Tarkin had drawn love hearts all around the mermaid. It was a good drawing. She looked pretty with lots of shells around her neck, masses of long dark hair and a blue and green fish tail. Magnus was delighted. He had told Tarkin at playtime about his birthday. Maybe this was an early birthday present.

Then Tarkin wrote the words *Wot she sayin?* in his jotter and pushed it across to Magnus Fin.

Mrs McLeod had turned her back to the class and was unrolling a huge map of Scotland. She pointed out where the world surfing championships were usually held, right up at the top in Thurso.

"Here you get the best waves – great big things. But now? Now girls and boys? Flat as a tattie scone."

Magnus Fin wrote *sea dying* and pushed it back to Tarkin. Then both boys stared up at the map of Scotland with worried faces. Mrs McLeod suddenly stopped talking, her mouth fell open and she stared down at Magnus Fin's desk. The picture of the mermaid surrounded by many large red love hearts had caught her attention.

"This is a serious matter, Magnus Fin. Fish are dying. The waves have stopped. And you doodle a mermaid. Mermaid! For heaven's sake! Pupils in P6 should know the difference between fantasy and reality. Mermaids don't exist. And if we don't do something about it, fish won't either."

"Sure mermaids exist. I saw one – in Alaska – and she was awesome," Tarkin said, not knowing he was supposed to put his hand up if he wanted to say something.

"Oh, right then, well why don't you tell the whole class what this *mermaid* looked like, Tarkin?" said Mrs McLeod, rubbing her hands together as though she was cold, or getting ready for a fight.

"Sure," he said, standing up and facing the class. "Well, guys, like I said, she was totally awesome. I'm in Alaska and it's wintertime, right? Dad has taken me fishing – Mom and Dad were still together back then, and we are just not catching a thing and it is freezing, like, totally ice. I've got on this big fur coat we found in the cellar of this old house we were renting. That was, like, house number ten. So we're on this lake and Dad gets out his flask and we're drinking coffee and just letting the boat drift across the water and you can see your breath making smoke signals in the air. I tell you it's so cold. Oh, man, even with that bear round my shoulders I am *freezing*. I'm ice."

"Tarkin, I think we understand you were cold," said Mrs McLeod.

"OK, yeah, well, we are just drifting and the moon comes up and suddenly I hear this sound. I think it's a fish jumping. I turn and there she is, a mermaid. She has long black hair and shining skin and a necklace with shells and pearls. I stare at her like I'm totally struck dumb, and she stares at me, and my heart's hopping like a rabbit. She is beautiful. Then I don't know why but I shout out, "Dad – look!" and as soon as I do she disappears under the water. I wish I'd never shouted out. She never came up again. For ages we waited for her to come back. And I didn't want to drop any more hooks under the water in case we hurt her. Well, we got too cold and Dad said we had to go back – he said I'd see her again one day. Well, I ain't never forgotten her and I never will. Ever."

Then Tarkin folded his arms and sat down, and for a while the class was silent. Mrs McLeod coughed and sat on her desk. For a second it seemed as if she was stumped for words.

"Right then," she said, suddenly standing up. "Well. Tarkin is a really good storyteller, isn't he, P6? Well, thank you, Tarkin. So, um … when we do our beach clean-up before the summer holidays we might see a mermaid. Or we might not! Alaska is a long way away. Who can tell me where Alaska is?"

Tarkin mouthed the answer to Magnus Fin who shot up his hand. "The USA, Miss!" he said.

"Yes, very good, Magnus. Some people think it's in Canada but it's not. Right then, off you go, P6. And don't forget to do your homework – name ten different kinds of fish and draw them!"

Chapter Seven

"Like I said, Fin, I've seen a lot, but nothing as cool as this." Tarkin whistled as Magnus handed him cowrie shells and coloured stones and bird skulls that day after school. "You're right – real treasure – wow!"

"Look at this one," said Magnus, handing Tarkin a metal sign that had the word BALLROOM etched on it. "My best one ever. It must have come off a sunken ship. I think it's from the *Titanic*." The two boys were sitting on the floor in Magnus Fin's room and Magnus pinched himself twice to check he wasn't dreaming.

Tarkin took the treasure in his hands and turned the sign around and around, his eyes wide with wonder. "Phew! Awesome! Man, I think you're right. This *is* from the *Titanic*. It hit an iceberg, right? And the musicians just kept on playing even when the ship was sinking. Wow! I wonder what kind of dances they did in the ballroom. Or did they play ball in the ballroom? You could get a fortune for this, Fin – you could be rich."

"I want to keep it," he said, hoping Tarkin would give the sign back soon. He felt nervous the way Tarkin kept turning it over and over. "It's my favourite treasure. You're the first person to see it except me. Granny saw the toilet sign but not this one. This is my very best treasure."

"You're right, Fin," said Tarkin, handing back the precious sign. "Who cares about being rich? This is the best thing ever. Most kids buy stuff down at the store – you get the best things down at the shore! That is so cool."

After he had shown Tarkin his favourite treasures he took out the drawing of the mermaid. "She's the prize," said Magnus Fin. He stood on his bed then Sellotaped the mermaid picture on to his wall so she would be the first thing he would see when he woke up. Tarkin grinned and nodded his head.

"Great story you told us at school," Magnus Fin said, wanting to hear more about the beautiful mermaid. But Tarkin said if you talk too much about magical glimpses you might not be given more.

"Yeah but how do you know it was a mermaid you saw? It could have been a girl. I mean, you didn't see her tail, did you?" Magnus Fin said, but Tarkin just pointed to his lips and made a zipping gesture. When Fin saw that his friend had no more to say on the subject of mermaids he resumed rummaging in his treasure chest.

"Well, look at this. This is a bit of anchor from a pirate ship," he said, handing Tarkin a piece of rusty iron.

"Wow, Fin, it's real heavy. Pirates are so cool. Hey," he said, putting a hand over one eye for an eye patch and hobbling around the room, ringing the bell and limping as though he had a wooden leg, "I'm Long John Silver."

Suddenly he stopped his pirate impersonation, swung round and said, "How come you live with your great-grand-parents? They are just so ancient, man." Tarkin had caught a glimpse of Barbara as she shuffled off to the bathroom – without her face scarf – and the boys had passed through the living room, where Tarkin had spotted Ragnor asleep by the fire.

Magnus Fin took back the anchor and coughed. It was possible that Tarkin didn't know. Everyone in the village knew that Ragnor and Barbara were Magnus Fin's strange parents, but perhaps word had not yet reached the new boy from America. Magnus didn't like telling lies, but it came out anyway. It felt easier that way.

"Oh yeah, um, my mum and dad and, yeah, even my grandparents – they all drowned at sea," he said, feeling his cheeks flame.

"Woah," said Tarkin, "I've never met a boy with dead parents before."

"Right, well, how do you like my new cormorant's skull. Found it last week," Magnus Fin said, shoving his prize skull into his new friend's hands.

"So, you are like, an orphan?" Tarkin asked, studying the fine white skull. "Man, that is just so way-out. I didn't know they still had orphans. You could live with us when the G-G-Ps kick the bucket; that'd be so cool. My mom wouldn't mind a bit. I don't think."

"Um … right, OK then. Um, so what is G-G-Ps?"

"Great-grand-parents. I just made it up." Tarkin grinned and did his impersonation of an old man with a walking stick. Fin, even though he felt bad about lying, laughed.

"So, what about your parents, Tarkin?"

"Oh! Well, Dad's a sculptor. He makes things out of wood. Dad got sick of moving all the time. He still lives in the Yukon." Tarkin grew silent for a moment, turned the bird skull in his hands then coughed and carried on, "And Mom was a singer in a band. Till she damaged her throat that was, so now she's having a go at milking goats and writing musicals. She really loves it here but she says that about everywhere. This is the fourteenth place I've lived. Whitehorse in the Yukon was the best – man, but it was so cold!"

Magnus Fin could listen to Tarkin for hours. He knew nothing about all the places this boy from America spoke about: the foreign countries, bands, art, high-rise buildings, huge shopping malls, tepee's, music festivals, magic spells. Magnus Fin had never been out of Scotland and seldom out of the village.

But Tarkin could also listen to Magnus Fin for hours as he talked about his shells, how he found a baby dogfish in a rock pool, how he spent hours and hours in the summer swimming, diving and fishing, how he was always looking for treasures from sunken ships and gathering driftwood to build fires on the beach. How he loved watching the birds by the sea, the fulmars and gannets and shags and cormorants and how, best of all, he loved diving with his mask and snorkel, and how once he'd swum with dolphins and once come face to face underwater with a seal.

Magnus Fin had found a friend at last. And if the sound of his mother sobbing came from the next room he could now just think, *Poor old G-G-P!*

Chapter Eight

Magnus Fin and Tarkin became the best of friends. Having G-G-Ps in the house made Magnus Fin's problem so much easier to bear, and everything with Tarkin was fun. Even school was more exciting, and now that Magnus had a friend the other children looked at him differently. Even Sandy Alexander, the class bully, stopped tripping him up in gym and pushing him into the lockers. Some children were even friendly to him.

"So it does get hot here," said Tarkin one sunny lunchtime when they were both sitting in the playground, munching each other's sandwiches and feeling the hot sun burn their faces. "Mom says if the weather stays like this she'll be happy to live in Scotland for ever. I really hope it does. I'm sick of moving."

"What about snow?" said Magnus Fin, remembering the previous winter and how he had built an enormous snowman that hadn't melted for two weeks. He turned to look at his friend while picking out the gherkin Tarkin's mother had put in with the cheese.

"Yeah. Snow. Right. Don't think Mom will go for snow. In the Yukon she never came outside. Just me and Dad went fishing. She watched reality TV all day."

"All day?"

"Twenty-four seven."

"Tell me about the mermaid again?"

"No."

"Go on, Tarkin. Please. And I'll give you my wetsuit and let you dive in the wreck."

"For real?" Tarkin's eyes lit up.

"Yeah. Promise."

"Deal. OK. Well, she called my name and she had the most awesome voice you could imagine. And I said, "Dad, do you hear her? She's saying 'Tarkin'. She's saying my name." But Dad couldn't hear her so that's how I know she was magic and I had the ears to hear the magic. I think one day I'll marry her, but if I talk too much about her the magic won't happen. I read that in a book in Australia. You ever heard that, Fin, about keeping quiet about magic?"

Magnus Fin shook his head. "Do you think I could marry her too?"

"No, Fin. You can't have two boys marrying one girl. But maybe you'll find another one. You never seen one? You sure?"

Magnus Fin shook his head again.

"So when we going diving, Fin?"

"Tonight?" Magnus Fin said. "Cos it's so hot. The sea's better when it's hot. You'll love it."

At seven o'clock that night the two boys ran down to the beach, Tarkin wearing Magnus Fin's wetsuit. Tarkin was taller than Magnus so his thin legs stuck out the bottom and the arms only went as far as his elbows.

"Lucky for us the water's warm," said Magnus Fin, giggling at the sight of Tarkin in the wetsuit. "Come on, race you. The sunken ship is past the rocks." And the two boys ran over the sand, yelling and shouting. Tarkin looked like some kind of black and white gangly octopus the way his arms and legs flapped about. Even his ponytail bouncing up and down looked like another tentacle.

"Hey, Fin, I can't run with this rubber stuff on. Whee! I look like a deep-sea diver."

"Here it is," said Magnus, who won the race for once. "Can you see the mast? It's that black stick thing out there. Well, that's the mast of the sunken fishing boat. I've been down there loads of times. I've already got most of the treasure from it but there's still a compass floating about attached to a bit of wire. Maybe you can get that, Tarkin? Here's a knife. All you've got to do is dive down, breathe through the snorkel, cut the wire, grab the compass and swim back up. Easy peasy!" But Tarkin didn't look so sure. His fair skin turned even paler.

"Sure," he said, twisting his ponytail round and round his finger, "sounds cool."

"You said you were a great swimmer, Tarkin. You'll be fine. It's not far and the tide's out. Find some bit of the boat to hold on to so you don't float up."

Tarkin still looked pale. He bit his bottom lip and shrugged his shoulders, then seemed to find confidence from somewhere. "Sure, man. I *am* a great swimmer. Man – I am the best. The *best*. Hi-fives." And they slapped each other's hands.

With that Tarkin waded out into the water, adjusted his mask, flung himself under with an enormous splash then disappeared. Magnus Fin started counting.

After ten seconds Tarkin was up again, puffing away as though he had just swum the channel. "Wow! Wow that was so cool. I went under, Fin, I went right under and I saw the boat and I could breathe. I opened my eyes. With this mask I could see right under the water. Wow! It's all broken up and full of seaweed but you can still see it's a boat. Wow! You don't get that in New York!"

"Did you get the compass?"

"No. That was just a check. Man, you gotta know, you don't go for treasure without doing a check first. OK, I'm off again. You are the greatest Fin, giving me your wetsuit and this ultra cool mask." Once again Tarkin threw himself into the water and with a yell and a splash he vanished.

Magnus Fin, standing neck high in the water, started counting again: 17–18–19–20–21 …

As he did he felt something nudge his ankles … 28–29–30 … He thought it was a frond of seaweed but after five more seconds it came again, a thick warm nudge this time against his knees. Still counting, Magnus Fin felt about in the water … 46–47–48 … His hand brushed something sleek and warm. Whatever it was, it moved. Suddenly the great head of a seal raised itself above the water and stared into Magnus Fin's eyes, not three inches away. The seal's eyes were a glistening sea green, and kind, and concerned. The seal didn't open its mouth but it was as if Magnus heard the creature speak.

"Quick! Your friend is in danger. Save him. Quick!" And as silently as it had appeared the seal lowered its gentle dog-like head and vanished from sight.

In an instant Magnus Fin dived down into the water and swam as fast as he could towards the wreck. And sure enough there was Tarkin under the water kicking and thrashing and sinking. Magnus kicked his ankles, swam underneath Tarkin, swung his friend's thrashing arm over his own shoulder, and in three strokes brought Tarkin back up to the surface. In seconds he had Tarkin lying tummy down on the beach, beating his back.

"Tarkin!" he shouted as he pummelled, his voice choked with fear and worry, "*Tarkin!*"

These seconds dragged like long, awful minutes. Magnus Fin's heart pounded in his chest. Tears stung his eyes. Suddenly, with a great gasp and a heave, Tarkin lifted his head and a gallon of seawater gushed out of his lungs. Magnus cried out and continued pummelling his friend's back. Tarkin, too, cried out then he struggled to sit up, his face white as a sheet and streaming with water.

"I'm really sorry, Tarkin," Magnus Fin gasped. "I thought you were doing fine. I didn't know. Something brushed my legs. A seal. I think it was a seal. Then I knew you were in danger. You were drowning." The words tumbled out. Shaking, relieved words.

"Thanks, Fin. You saved me. I can't swim. I just said I could. I can't. I can't dive. I wanted to. Oh

God, I nearly drowned." Magnus Fin couldn't tell what were tears and what was seawater, it was all salty and streaming down Tarkin's face.

"I thought you could swim. Tarkin, I thought you were a great swimmer?"

"No. I thought if I tried maybe I could. I just said that to myself." His panting and gasping stopped. Tarkin looked at his friend, and Magnus thought he had never seen such a sad look from a boy. "We never hang around anywhere long enough for me to go to lessons. I want to swim. I really want to, Fin."

"Well, at least you're safe now." Magnus slapped his friend on the back. The two boys laughed and laughed out of sheer relief, not knowing that just behind them a beautiful seal lifted her head out of the water, for a second stared at them, then lowered herself back into the sea.

Chapter Nine

That following Sunday, the day of Magnus Fin's eleventh birthday, something happened to change his life for ever. Since his parents' aging, birthdays were very much like any other day – or they had been – until now. Magnus Fin remembered years earlier, when he was three years old, his mother had baked a cake and given him presents. She had sung happy birthday and danced about the small cottage. He remembered his father gave him a mini-surfboard. Those had been happy days.

"Happy birthday, Magnus Fin," he said to himself, stretching and gazing at his mermaid picture. He would make the day special for himself in some way: go to the beach and see what the tide had brought in; eat a huge bag of pick-and-mix sweets then go to his favourite rock pool; perhaps take Tarkin to his favourite rock pool. He put his surf shorts on and went through to the kitchen to make his breakfast.

"Happy birthday, son," said his father, "I've got a present for you." Ragnor was up and dressed. He seemed excited and nervous. Magnus Fin felt the excitement transfer to him till a shudder ran up his spine. Suddenly he remembered – the story! Today he would hear this strange story. His heart missed a beat. Normally he enjoyed his breakfast cereal, but today he couldn't eat.

"I want you to come with me to the cave," continued his father, "soon as you're ready. Remember I told you? Well, son, now you're eleven, it's time for the story."

"I'm ready," Magnus Fin said, pushing aside his bowl of untouched Rice Krispies. The thought crossed his mind whether, now he was eleven, he should still be eating Rice Krispies, or should he be having something grown-up instead, like muesli? Tarkin ate muesli.

Magnus Fin was at the front door in two minutes. He could feel his eleven-year-old heart thudding in his ribs. He was trembling with fear and excitement. He loved stories, but somehow he felt that this birthday story would not be like the other stories. "You'll be shocked," that's what his father had said. Magnus Fin's stomach was a flutter of butterflies.

Just as father and son were about to leave the house they heard Barbara call out from her bedroom, "Magnus. Happy birthday, Magnus."

"Give her a hug, son," Ragnor said, "go on."

Magnus Fin ran through to where his mother lay propped up in bed. "Here is the best present," she said, reaching over to her son and giving him a warm hug. Magnus Fin smiled at his mother, for once not seeing the aged face but only the warm brown eyes. Then he ran out to where his father stood at the garden gate.

"Come on then, birthday boy," said his father, and the two of them set off for the cave. The sun was already high in the sky and sparkling on the water. Ragnor's cave was a good twenty-minute walk along the shore at the slow pace he walked.

The cave was deep enough to shelter from the rain and wind, and there was many a day that Ragnor sought out his beach cave. No one knew what he did there, and though there were rumours enough, no one from the village ever came to find out. The truth was he sat there, he made fires there, he gazed out to sea there, he sang his old songs and sometimes he slept there. In the old days he and Barbara had done their courting there, but nowadays this cave was a place Ragnor went to be alone.

Magnus Fin watched his father limp across the rocks while he himself jumped lightly from stone to stone. He wondered if Ragnor would ever make it. On the sand they walked side by side and eventually reached the mouth of the cave.

Magnus Fin stared in. It had changed since the last time he was there. His father had made a seat from stones. There was even a small stone table and in the middle of the cave there was a dug-out fireplace surrounded by a circle of stones. Everything was neat. There were natural shelves in the cave where the rock jutted inwards. Here Ragnor had placed stubs of candle and circles of shells. There was even, Magnus noticed, what looked like a drawing of a seal or mermaid on the cave wall. Fin had never seen it before. Perhaps he had never looked closely enough – or perhaps they had come to a different cave.

"It's cosy in here," said Magnus. "You've got it like home, Dad."

"It is in a way. And it's fine and quiet. Sit yourself down, son," Ragnor said, nodding in the direction of the stone seat. For a long time Ragnor didn't speak. Magnus Fin sat on the seat and waited. His father arranged driftwood into a spire then sparked the dry wood into life. It crackled and soon a strip of smoke curled up and wafted towards the mouth of the cave.

"Rare smell, isn't it?" Ragnor said, sitting on the stone table because there was only one seat. Magnus Fin nodded. It was.

Through the smoke Magnus Fin peered at his father, thinking he had never seen anyone so lined, so grey. "I wasn't always this way," Ragnor said, reading his thoughts. "This ancient-looking creature you see is not me. You could say that what you see is an enchantment. And now it's your eleventh birthday. It's a special age, son – no longer a young boy, not yet a man. Some call it the age between the worlds. Listen to me carefully, my son, while I tell you – I wasn't always a human man."

The smoke stung Magnus Fin's eyes. He rubbed them, thinking in that moment he might faint, or run away, or cry. What was his father saying? What kind of a birthday gift was this? Where was the mountain bike or the surfboard? This bent and lined man sitting opposite him and now staring at him through the smoke – who was he? And what did he mean – enchantment?

"It's time you knew the truth about where you came from, Magnus Fin. Let me tell you as best I can: the green eye you got from me and the sea, the brown eye you got from your mother and the land. And the deep blue pupils in your eyes you got from your grandmother, the wisest and most beautiful seal that ever lived. These stories we told you, Fin, about me being a fisherman from a far-off island – they weren't true, or not completely. Aye, Fin, even your name has a claim to both worlds. Magnus was given to you from your mother after her father. Fin you got from me, and the sea. I can tell you the truth now, son; great Neptune knows I've carried it in me long enough – my secret, like a weight around my neck. I am – or, I was – a selkie."

Magnus Fin swallowed then shivered and rubbed his hands together, even though it was warm by the flames of the fire. *Selkie!* He'd heard that word before – in a story maybe. But now his head was in a spin. What was his father saying – he was a selkie? Feeling dizzy he remembered the sea shanty he'd often heard his father sing.

I am a man upon the land
I was a selkie in the sea
But I came ashore and married a lass
Now I'll see no more my Sule Skerrie.

His father went on with his tale and it took Magnus Fin all his strength not to fall from the stone chair. "You'll have heard of us, son, or maybe not. I am a seal man, a selkie. Man on the land, seal in the water. It's not given to all seals but there are some of us with the gift of both worlds. When the moon was full I could slip out of my seal skin and take on the form of a man. We selkies had fun, I can tell you. Sometimes we would hide our seal skins and go to dances when we heard music

playing on the land, and human folk would say
we could dance like the waves of the sea. Little
knowing it was the waves of the sea taught us to
dance in the first place. Aye, I lived out there, far
out there and way down deep. I come from a place
called the Emerald Valley of the seal people, or, in
our ancient tongue, Sule Skerrie. I miss it, son,
more than you can ever know."

Magnus Fin hadn't fainted, or fallen from his
stone seat. He sat rigid as though he himself
was made of stone. He didn't know what to say.
A tear ran from his father's eyes. Maybe this
was not a time for Magnus to speak. He twisted
his hands together and stared into the fire. The
strange words his father was speaking continued
unravelling like thread.

"I was a handsome, fit and brave seal. Oh, Fin,
I could swim faster than any seal – no whale could
ever catch me – but I was also foolish. It was
sport amongst us young selkies to try for a human
girlfriend. A kiss from a human girl, for us in our
world, was like kissing a beautiful princess in this
world. And, Fin, your mother was a beauty. You
can't see that now, and we are both to blame for
that, but your granny has told you often enough
how beautiful she was and it's true. I used to
watch her picking shells on the shore. Sometimes
she swam in the sea. Once she lay on a rock in the
sun and that's when I kissed her. I slipped out of
my seal skin, bent over her as she slept and kissed
her. Then I brought her jewels that I had taken
from the holds of wrecked ships. Son, you wouldn't
believe what riches are under the sea!"

For a second Magnus Fin's troubled mind flitted to his own Neptune's Cave. Yes, he knew what treasure there was under the sea. He nodded at his father but Ragnor was staring into the smoke of the fire.

"Your mother found me handsome and of course she liked the jewels I brought her. She said I was far more pleasing than any crofter or farmer's son. I loved her beauty and though all the selkies warned me against it I came ashore and married her. I gave her my seal skin and took on a human form for I couldn't bear to live without her. You were born, Fin, and we loved you dearly – though your eyes unsettled your mother."

Magnus Fin blinked. He could imagine his eyes unsettled his mother.

"For three years, Fin, we were blissfully happy. Folk in the village often said they'd never met a couple more in love than we were."

Magnus Fin listened to his father's words. He had always known he was somehow different, and he had always loved the sea. He, Magnus Fin, was descended from the seal folk. It made sense, in a strange dream-like way, and it frightened him to the core. Questions, that for so long now he had sewn up inside himself, came tumbling out: "But how did you know how to be a man? I mean, do you feel like a seal inside yourself? How did you learn to talk? How did you take off your skin? How?"

"Oh, lad, so many questions. Us selkies know both worlds. It was easy for me to be a man because I had often taken off my skin. You could say this stay on the land has just gone on for longer than usual. Anyway, Fin, on your third birthday I wanted to take you under the sea. It is our custom to present our young to the family at the age of three. Us seal folk have always done this. It's a time of great celebration and well-wishing. It's the time the young one meets the elders and good wishes are given, we call them hansels."

Magnus Fin stared at his father through the flames of the fire. The words he was hearing had a strange effect on him. Part of him wanted to listen, part of him wanted to run away. But, taking deep breaths, he continued listening to his father's tale.

"I begged your mother to give me back my seal skin. I promised I would only be gone for three days, but your mother was petrified I would go and take you and we would never return, and she'd be left alone. I tried to convince her, Fin, but the truth is I couldn't convince even myself. I wasn't sure that, once under the sea and back with my own folks, I would ever come back. Barbara knew that, Fin, and on that day she took out my seal skin and she burnt it."

Magnus Fin gasped. "She didn't mean to," his father added quickly. "She has told me that a thousand times. It was only meant to be a tiny burn, just enough to make it difficult for me to live for more than a few days underwater. But she had forgotten how dry the seal skin had become. Four years out of the salt water and my seal skin was dry as tinder. When she held a match to it the whole thing went up in flames. I begged her to stop. I felt the flames burn me as though my seal skin was still a part of me. The fire seared through my legs. I screamed. She screamed."

A shiver ran the length of Magnus Fin's spine. "She tried to stamp it out," his father went on, "and doing so she burnt her foot. Since that day I have limped and she has limped. And since that day, Fin, every year has been as seven to your mother and me. Under the sea, the tides renew us, the waves keep us young. We selkies live hundreds of years. But here on the land I took on human time and lived as a human man, but after the burning of my skin everything changed. With the burning of the skin we broke the law of the sea and every day we age, we grow greyer, weaker, slower."

"But if she is sorry, I mean, if Mum didn't mean to, can't she be forgiven? We can all do things that are wrong, can't we? We don't have to suffer for years and years, do we? Is there nothing that can be done to help?" Magnus Fin's eyes were wide with anguish.

"If the waves came back that might help in some way, son. We used to bathe in the sea, your mum and me. It helped but she always clung on to me, afraid I might dive under the water and never come back. Little did she know I couldn't even swim without my seal skin. But you can, Fin. So now, son, I have told you my story. Uncommon though it is, it is your story too. Had you received the hansels that were yours by right at the age of three, you would have had the bravery to stand up to anyone. I'm sorry, Fin – you've had to cope without the good wishes of your seal kin."

"What is a hansel?" asked Magnus Fin.

"Well now, every young selkie needs a hansel. It's a gift, Fin – a good wish for your life from your ancestors. It's our way of passing on good things to the young. You missed them when you were three. And so I couldn't speak of this until you turned eleven years old – the year between the ages when you are both child and man. So often I longed to, for look, Fin, can you see how weak the sea has become? Have you not wondered what has happened to the waves? I fear for my people, Fin. Look, the tide is far out, let me show you something."

Magnus Fin, as though in a dream, got up from his stone seat, left the cave and followed his father. A black-backed gull wheeled overhead. The sea was glass still. The tide was low. It was true: the waves were small and weak as though they were hardly able to drive themselves up the shore. Climbing over the black and seaweed-strewn rocks, Magnus Fin thought with every tottering step that his father would slip and fall. It seemed an age that they clambered over them.

Magnus Fin's head spun like a leaf in the wind. Thoughts whizzed like electric shocks through his brain till he felt his head would burst. If his father was a selkie, what did that make him? What would Tarkin say if he found out? Was his father going mad? Tarkin said old folk can get senile. Was Dad senile – so that now he believed in selkies? They don't exist, do they? Do they? Do they?

"What's that, son?" Ragnor asked, still shuffling carefully over seaweed-strewn rocks. Magnus had been speaking his thoughts and his doubts. "Do they what?" Magnus Fin couldn't speak. The story he had heard in the cave shook him to his depths. Nothing was certain any more. His parents were freaks. And what did that make him – with one green eye and one brown eye, blue pupils, webbed feet and a father from under the sea? An alien!

"Aye, son," came his father's voice, "they do."

For some reason these definite words spoken by his father gave Magnus Fin some feeling of comfort. They stopped his world from breaking. "They do, they do," he repeated to himself, trying to still his thumping heart. Selkies exist, mermaids exist, magic exists!

They reached the water line and Ragnor stopped at a black and jagged rock. Magnus Fin knew the shore like he knew his own hands and this large black rock that jutted far out to sea was only visible at low tide. Where they stood now was mostly underwater.

"Look, Fin," said Ragnor, bending over and gesturing towards a cluster of shells in the shape of a crescent moon on the side of the black rock, half submerged in water. "This is the handle of a door. Without my seal skin I can't go through the door to the world under the sea but you can, son. At the age of eleven a child born of land and sea is granted the ability to live in both worlds. It's granted to few, Fin – very few."

Magnus Fin swallowed hard. He didn't know what to say. If he was supposed to feel brave and strong, now that he was eleven, he didn't. In fact it was all he could do to stop his knees shaking. His father looked at him then looked again at the shell handle at the side of the black rock.

"At low tide when the moon is full, return here, Fin, and it will open for you. They will be waiting for you, Fin. Your grandmother will guide you. It's time for you to meet your people and get your hansels. I failed to take you when you were three. Now you are eleven, you must make the journey under the sea alone."

While his father was speaking Magnus Fin stared down through the water. When the wavy seaweed fronds swayed to one side he could see the handle of shells. It didn't look like a door, though the crescent of shells did look like a handle. His heart thumped. He imagined himself coming to this place, diving into the water and opening this door. Where would it take him? He had heard of doors to other worlds. Was there another world behind this simple cluster of shells?

"Tell them Ragnor sent his son. Say you've come for the hansels at last." With those words Ragnor limped over the rocks and made his way back to the beach, leaving Magnus Fin staring at the handle at the place where the land meets the sea. Then, as though someone had suddenly snapped their fingers in front of his face, the boy jerked his head up. For a moment he felt alone, utterly alone. Then he turned and saw the figure of his father bending down in the distance. The old man was lifting something from the beach. "Fin!" he called, waving his son over.

Magnus Fin leapt over the rocks to where his father now stood on the sand. Ragnor held a stone up, its white and orange veins flashing in the sunlight. He handed the stone to his son.

"For you, Fin," he said. "It's a moon-stone. We say it gives protection and courage. It might help you. Happy birthday, son." Fin took the round stone. The sea had worn a hole in the middle of it. It felt warm and good in the palm of his hand. "I'll find a leather lace and you can wear it round your neck," Ragnor said, tired now and resting on a rock. "Run off and play now, lad, while I get my breath."

Magnus Fin ran off along the shore. The sea was flat, good for skimming. He found flat stones and skimmed them eight, nine then ten times over the still water. "Hey, I've broken my record," he yelled, suddenly happy now. Despite what his father had just asked him to do, an excitement and happiness bubbled inside him. He clutched his birthday stone. He wouldn't skim that. He kept that in his pocket, like gold.

That night, in the dark comfort of his own Neptune's Cave, Magnus Fin decided he would go on this strange journey. He would wait seven days until the moon was full then he would find that shell handle again and pull it. And probably nothing would happen.

Tarkin said there were loads of crazy people in the world. Magnus didn't want to believe it, but it seemed his old father was going mad. Magnus Fin fell asleep that birthday night, wondering if he would tell Tarkin about this or not.

And what if it *was* true? What if he really *did* have a grandmother with a tail waiting for him behind the door to the sea?

Chapter Ten

Those seven days before full moon were shot through with an arrow of trembling anticipation. When Magnus Fin thought about the door to the world under the sea at low tide, a shiver ran up his spine. His father, after the great deal of talking on Magnus Fin's birthday, was now even more silent than usual. He went slowly about his business: catching fish, mending his net, helping his wife gut and cook the fish, banking up the fire, then bringing Barbara cups of tea in bed and nodding off in front of the fire.

Barbara kept the cottage noisy with the constant buzz of her television or radio programmes. Sometimes she chuckled to herself and sometimes she moaned. On several occasions Magnus Fin wondered if his parents were going mad and then realised, here was he, about to try and open a door to the world under the sea. He was as mad as they!

Two days before full moon, Magnus Fin sat in the familiar comfort of his room, surrounded by his treasures from the sea. He examined everything carefully lest he should never see it again. "Help me, fishing nets, *Titanic* ballroom sign, anchor from the pirate ship, conch shell, killer-whale bone, cormorant skull, coloured stones, prehistoric pottery, horseshoe from Norway, life ring from

Poland, plastic boat from Shetland, blue glass, penny from 1957, silver wedding ring, and mermaid picture, help me." The house was quiet now, apart from the clock in the kitchen tick-tocking and the scratching sound of Barbara's radio, barely audible.

Magnus Fin was on his way to the kitchen to make himself a hot chocolate. His father was in his chair by the fire but not asleep. Ragnor looked up at him, those shining emerald-green eyes still young despite the wizened face surrounding them. Magnus met his gaze and could tell his father was thinking about the door at the black rock, counting down the days till full moon.

"And how is it to be eleven?" his father asked him, looking up and smiling.

"It's fine," said Magnus Fin, "and I think my last baby tooth is wobbly." Father and son grinned at each other and the nervousness Magnus felt melted away. He was looking forward to his adventure now. If he was half selkie, he might find great treasures from sunken ships! And his dad had said he wouldn't need a snorkel to breathe underwater. He'd find far greater treasures than any he gathered at the seashore.

The day before full moon, Tarkin came round to Magnus Fin's house after school. He had noticed the shining stone his friend wore round his neck and he wanted one too.

"Let's go along the shore and look for one," Magnus suggested. So they did. They searched for ages, and though there were many round stones, white stones, marble stones, orange stones and shining stones, they couldn't find one with a perfect hole in the middle of it. Tarkin grew bored.

"Hey, Fin, let's find crabs instead," he suggested. Magnus Fin loved crabs, especially tiny velvet crabs. He took Tarkin to the rock pool where his favourite crabs lived and for ages the boys stared at the small scuttling creatures in amongst the red and purple seaweed. Then Tarkin ran off, shouting for Magnus Fin to come and see who was the best stone skimmer. Magnus had a quick action with his wrist and, from years of practice, he was by far the champion stone skimmer.

"My mum is not really a singer in a band; I mean, she never was," Tarkin suddenly blurted out, throwing a stone over the flat sea and managing three skims. "She sells candles. I think, like, when she was eighteen, she once sang a few songs in some smutty dive in Las Vegas. And my dad isn't a sculptor. He works in a factory somewhere and hasn't written to me for two years. So, now you know the truth. I'm glad I told you," he said, looking relieved.

Magnus Fin knew that this was his moment – if they were coming clean about parents. But how could he say it? He hadn't thought twice about Tarkin's mum and had forgotten she was supposed to have been a singer in a band anyway.

"So, don't you want to tell me anything, Fin?" Tarkin asked, smiling encouragement at his friend. The villagers must have told him, word must have got round. It was bound to sooner or later. It was always going to be a matter of time before the new family learnt the truth about the weird ones down by the shore. Magnus Fin felt caught in a web of lies. He blurted out, "I know a secret door."

He hadn't meant to say anything about the door, but he felt so bad about pretending he was an orphan, he needed to change the subject. Tarkin's eyes lit up. "Wow! Like where, Fin? Where?"

The tide was coming in. The black rock was hidden under the water. The door would be inaccessible. "Come to the cave and I'll tell you," said Magnus Fin, running now along the beach with Tarkin following him.

The two boys sat in the place where, not a week before, Magnus Fin and his father had sat. Magnus made a fire, just as his father had done.

"This place is so cool," said Tarkin, gazing around the cave, thinking he had landed up on some film set where pirates would appear any moment and he'd finally get to meet Johnny Depp. "Hey, why did you never bring me here before, Fin? It is seriously cool."

Magnus Fin took a deep breath and peered at his friend through the smoke. "Because this is my father's cave," he said. Tarkin immediately glanced round, expecting to see a skeleton in the corner, or a ghost. "Yes," Magnus went on, "I mean, he's still alive and he's different from most people and – um – well ... I suppose I am too." Magnus Fin stopped. His friend was staring at him through the grey smoke. "Um, Tarkin, look ... do you believe in selkies?"

Chapter Eleven

The smoke from the fire in the cave swirled around so thickly that the boys had to peer to see each other and the smoke stung their eyes.

"Sure I believe in selkies," Tarkin said, rubbing his eyes and vigorously nodding his head, "sure I do. Man, I believe in everything. Mom says my imagination is highly developed. I believe in dragons too. You ever seen a dragon, Fin?" Magnus Fin shook his head.

"Well, you ever seen the Loch Ness Monster then?" Again Magnus Fin shook his head.

Tarkin carried on, his eyes growing wide and shiny as he spoke. "I know three boys in New York who have seen the Loch Ness Monster. They says they were really spooked out and she had bumps on her back. That's partly why we came here, to see it. I don't think it'll be the same as when I saw the mermaid. I think when I see the Loch Ness Monster it'll feel different. I might be frightened a bit but I don't care. Mom says it was the cold getting to my brain when I saw that mermaid, but Dad believes me. Fin, I know it was a real mermaid in Alaska and I'll never forget her. I fell in love with her."

Magnus Fin didn't want to wait unless he lost his courage. He blurted out as fast as he could, "My dad is a selkie, you know, a seal man, or he says so, or he was once, and he says I've got a grandmother at the other side of the door, and he says he comes from a valley under the sea called Sule Skerrie and he wants me to go there. And maybe he's crazy." The words hung in the smoky air, ashamed.

"Maybe he *was* a seal," said Tarkin, as though they were talking about school dinners or crabs or something ordinary. "Cool! So what about this door thing?" he asked, and Magnus immediately felt a rush of gratitude for this friend, who took all Magnus Fin's weirdness in his stride. He must have heard the strange stories in the village but he didn't seem to care.

"Maybe that mermaid you saw in Alaska, you know, the one you love, maybe she was a selkie," Magnus Fin said, his voice trembling with excitement.

"No, she was a mermaid."

"But how do you know, Tarkin? You didn't see her tail."

"I know, Fin. Some things you just know. Come on, man – I wanna know about the magic door!"

So, in the smoky cave, Magnus Fin told Tarkin everything his father had told him six days before. Tarkin listened, every now and then whistling or saying, "Cool!" When finally Magnus came to the end of his strange tale, Tarkin whistled again, extra long, and said, "I'll say a special chant I got from the Native Americans for you, Fin. How long do you think you'll be gone?"

Magnus Fin shrugged his shoulders then laughed. It all sounded so ridiculous. "About a minute, I think," he said, laughing. Then he kicked sand into the fire and ran out of the cave. "Hey, Tarkin! Want to race back along the shore?"

"OK, first to the sand is Superman," Tarkin said, speeding off with his ponytail bobbing up and down and his long, thin arms and legs pumping back and forth. Magnus was smaller than Tarkin and his legs had to go twice the speed to keep up. When they got to the sand they both fell down, panting and laughing.

"Want another skimming competition?" said Tarkin, scrambling to his feet and scooping up the flattest stones he could find. Magnus Fin was about to agree then changed his mind. If they threw stones out to sea they might hit a seal. They might hit his grandmother, or the seal that had saved Tarkin from drowning. Tarkin seemed to read his mind.

"Well, OK. How about we try to hit that plastic bottle over there?" he suggested instead.

So they gathered stones, made a marker and started to throw. "And if you step over the marker you're out," said Magnus Fin, watching Tarkin's toes edge over the line. Tarkin stepped back, took aim and threw. He missed. Magnus Fin focused on the bottle, stretched back his arm and threw with all his might. He missed.

"Tarkin? Do you think this, um, looking ancient thing – is it my fault?" Magnus Fin asked suddenly, in between shots.

"Man, no way. Let's face it, Fin, you would have really dug it – being three and going under the sea. How cool is that!"

Magnus Fin took aim and hit the plastic bottle. "Hey, Tarkin! I hit it! I hit it!"

"Good shot, Fin, good action. Just watch me." Tarkin aimed, threw, and missed. "Drat! Do you think Mom and Dad splitting up's my fault?"

"No way, Tarkin. You are the best ever. He probably misses you like mad." Magnus Fin smiled at his friend but Tarkin didn't smile back. Tarkin picked up another stone and Magnus wished Tarkin would hit the target.

He did. They both threw their arms in the air and yelled.

That night Magnus Fin studied the tide tables. Full moon was the next night at 10.25 pm. Low tide was between nine and midnight. His mother would be asleep. His father, he hoped, would be down at the cave, waiting.

With the bright moon shining in his window, it took Magnus Fin a very long time to fall asleep. When he did, he dreamt he had found the pearly handle in the rock, opened it – and there was nothing there.

Chapter Twelve

"Magnus Fin, if you can't stop staring out of the window you'll sit here and stare after the bell's gone. And what, may I ask, is so very interesting about the sky, hmm?"

Magnus Fin jolted his head down and fixed his eyes on the school book that lay open on his desk. For a second he couldn't remember what this lesson was supposed to be about. Was this maths? Was he expected to answer a sum? His school jotter told him nothing – the pages he was so intently staring at were blank.

"Seventeen, Miss," he blurted out, thinking it was better to say something than nothing at all. Mrs McLeod was always telling them how important it was to make an effort. It seemed, though, that this effort was not the kind she meant.

"Seventeen what? Sheep?" she asked. Now the whole class were staring at Magnus Fin and the girls at the back giggled behind their hands. "Seventeen baseball bats perhaps? Or, wait a minute, let me guess, is it seventeen clouds in the sky?"

"The Inuit people have at least seventeen words for snow, Miss." It was Tarkin, jumping in. He carried on, seeing that he had now caught Mrs McLeod's interest. She was staring at him, with his ponytail, tattoos and earrings, and now Inuit friends. "Yeah, and do you know, they play baseball too. You know I went to school in Whitehorse in the Yukon with real Inuit kids. They were so cool, Miss. One guy had a tattoo of a real cool polar bear across his back."

Mrs McLeod forgot about Magnus Fin and busied herself telling Tarkin that in Scotland it really was not the done thing to say "cool" all the time. "You need to expand your vocabulary," she said, her hands on her hips and her face turning pink. "How about wonderful, fantastic, amazing, braw, incredible, astounding, phenomenal, majestic, far-out even?" Tarkin told her "far-out" was a very uncool thing to say. Mrs McLeod gave up, by which time the school bell rang.

It was ten past three. Magnus Fin made a dash for the gate. Tarkin grabbed him by the sleeve as he whizzed past. "Hey, I'm with you all the way, Fin," he said, then let him go.

"Thanks, Tarkin, thanks, that's great," Magnus said, panting and looking flushed. His dark hair stood up like a brush and his eyes blazed: his green eye shone like emerald and his brown eye glistened like earth after rain.

Magnus Fin ran home, ate a bowl of hearty tomato soup that his mother had made then disappeared into his room. He took out each piece of treasure from sunken ships and lined them up around his bed. Then he wrote Tarkin a letter, saying if he, Magnus Fin, was never to return to the land, then Tarkin could have his treasures from the *Titanic* and thank you for being a great friend and he hoped very much that Tarkin would one day see his mermaid again and his dad.

Seconds felt like minutes. Magnus read snippets from the newspaper to his mother, but his mind was elsewhere – under the sea. Later he sat beside her and watched television, but could only see little coloured dots jumping in front of his eyes.

"Something's got you, son," she said in her small shaky voice. "Love, I bet. Eh? Is it? You can tell your mum. I might not look like much but I could turn a head or two." Barbara nudged him in the ribs, but Magnus Fin only shook his head. The truth was he was in love with the picture of the mermaid on his wall, but he could hardly tell his mother that.

Barbara sighed and said it was time for her bed. She turned to look at him. She had taken her face scarf off, saying it was too hot under that thing, and for a second he stared into her brown eyes. *Eyes*, he thought to himself, *don't seem to age*.

"Tell them I'm sorry," she whispered, then she got up and limped slowly off to her bedroom.

So his mother knew about his planned journey. She had tried once to stop someone she loved from going under the sea. Magnus Fin knew by the way she looked at him that she would never do that again. Her small words reverberated in his head – "Tell them I'm sorry" – and as he looked at her bent frame he wondered, would he ever see her again?

He stayed sitting on the sofa after his mother had gone, biting his nails and staring into the flames of the fire. At ten to ten his father nodded to him. It was time. Magnus Fin got up from the sofa, stared briefly at his father then ran through to his room.

Usually it took him ten minutes to reach the cave. Add another three or four for reaching the black rock, which gave him, he worked out, plenty of time. The moon would be full at 10.25 pm. He wanted to be there, ready to grasp the shell handle at quarter past.

Hands trembling, Magnus Fin pulled on his wetsuit then his trainers. He stretched then touched his toes. He felt fit, though wished he felt braver, and tried to ignore the butterflies in his stomach. Thinking of bravery he remembered his moon-stone. He had laid it carefully under his pillow the night before. He pulled the pillow back and stared. There was nothing there.

Panic rose in him. Where was it? Frantically he felt under the duvet, under the sheet. He dived under the bed and groped about over the carpet. His grasping hand touched shells, little boats he had made and bones – but no moon-stone. It was gone.

He wanted to burst into tears. He couldn't believe it. He had been so prepared and now the most important thing – his courage stone – was nowhere to be found. His heart sank remembering how granny had been in that afternoon. She had probably washed his bed sheets. He wanted to scream.

Frantically he searched in his treasure box, on his shelves, in the pages of his books, amongst his pieces of pottery. Maybe he hadn't left it under his pillow after all. Maybe he had put it in his school bag.

He tipped out the contents of his rucksack. The cormorant's skull was there but no moon-stone. Perhaps it was in the washing machine.

He ran through to the kitchen where his father was standing wringing his hands. "Go, Fin, just go, there's no time to lose," he said, his voice shaking.

"But – my courage stone," he cried, "I can't find it. I'm scared."

"Fin, you've only ten minutes, son. For the love of the sea, please go."

Fin's whole body was shaking. His knees were quaking, his lip quivering. Suddenly he felt so young. "I – I'm sorry."

The kitchen door opened. Fin spun round and there, with her long grey hair falling over her nightdress, was his mother. She stretched out a shaky hand towards him. "I found this in the washing basket," she said and opened her palm. There, nestled like a secret, was the moon-stone.

Fin's heart leapt. He scooped up the stone. It was still on its lace. Quick as lightning he tied it round his neck, took a deep breath, ran to the cottage door and laid his hand on the door handle. He had nine minutes before full moon.

"Good luck, son," his mother said. She lifted a bony hand and waved, a shadow of worry in her eyes. "Good luck."

Ragnor was by his side, his hand on the boy's shoulder, his face twisted with worry. "Quick, son, go – and run like the wind. It's now or never, please, Fin – go!"

Now Magnus Fin felt brave and strong. "Right,

Dad," he said, and like an athlete he dashed out of
the house. At the garden gate he looked back for a
second at the small cottage by the shore, thinking
he might never see it again. Then he turned and
sprinted to the beach.

As he ran, thoughts of his friend Tarkin flew
through his mind. Tarkin had said he'd be with
him all the way. Just knowing that put wings in
his feet.

He was breathing hard now, pumping his arms
back and forth and leaping over bracken and cow
parsley to take a shortcut to the beach path. A
buzzard soared overhead. It mewed like a cat, as
though willing him on. Racing down the beach
path to the rocks, Magnus Fin hoped that he,
Tarkin's best friend, could at least open a door in
the sea. If Tarkin was brave then so was Fin.

He reached the sandy beach in four minutes
then dashed along the shore to the cave. Pounding
the sand, he glanced at the underwater watch
Tarkin had given him. It was now 10.21 pm. He
had to reach the rock in four minutes. He pushed
himself on, though now his whole body ached and
his heart thumped. But the cave was in view now,
and there, jutting way out to sea, was the black
rock.

"Keep going," he willed himself, "keep going."
Running over the skerries he jumped on to a
green slimy rock, slipped and lost his footing. His
knee banged down on the stone. He cried out but
scrambled to his feet, not caring his knee was
throbbing, only caring he had two minutes left.

Magnus Fin's legs felt like lead. He would never

make it. He panted hard. The sight of the flat sea and the memory of his father's haunting story urged him on. He had to make it. There was no time to stop. No time to doubt.

Out to sea he ran now, leaping over rock pools and jutting stone, his heart thudding. He was almost there when a curlew trilled, making him glance round. Behind him a curl of smoke rose up from the mouth of the cave. It seemed to wave to him, to wish him luck. Magnus Fin, now feeling strong and confident, raised his hand and waved, then he raced forward again, jumping over the rocks like a goat.

His knee was sore. His legs were aching. The rocks were steep now. Gasping for breath he hoisted himself up.

One minute left. He must reach the handle in time. He must do what his father had begged him to do. Suddenly it was the most important thing in the world. He must meet his father's people under the sea.

Over the flat ocean he could see the huge face of the moon. In half a minute now it would be completely full. Tide, moon and boy had to coincide. This moment of crossing worlds had to be a moment between time – between the waxing and waning moon, between land and sea, between child and man. His heart hurt in his ribs it was knocking so hard.

He flung himself over the final rock pool and fell with a cry on to the black rock – and there it was in the swirling water beyond, half hidden behind fronds of seaweed: the glittering mother-of-pearl handle. With not a second to lose, Magnus Fin jumped into the cold water, reached out his hand through the tangle of seaweed and grasped it.

The handle gave under his touch. He pulled it through the water towards him. He felt the drag of a whirlpool. A crack flashed in the rock. A green emerald light blinked from the black, so bright it almost blinded him. And the door in the rock under the sea opened.

Chapter Thirteen

As the rock door opened, a tremendous sound crammed into the boy's ears, like a thousand screeching gulls. Magnus felt himself being sucked forward, pulled like a magnet. Something had brushed against him. Someone or something had taken him by the hand.

The emerald light was gone. The door closed behind him. Magnus Fin was floating now and water swirled around him and above him. His wetsuit clung to his skin and a warm, weightless feeling filled his body. Fronds of seaweed brushed his legs. He held his breath.

The slow ringing words, "Welcome, son of Ragnor," reverberated around him. In a daze, Magnus Fin looked around. Everything was filmy, swaying, like a dream. Who spoke? Who was holding his hand? Was he drowning? The voice sounded like bells, or flutes, or waves breaking. It soothed the boy. The voice and the hand soothed him.

"Welcome," it spoke again in a warm lilting voice, "you must be Ragnor's son." Magnus Fin felt as though he was dissolving, like sugar in tea, and wondered – had he drowned? Was he dead?

But the ringing voice sounded once more. "Welcome, son of Ragnor. I am your grandmother.

Welcome to the kingdom under the sea." And just when Magnus Fin couldn't hold his breath one second longer, a kiss pressed against his lips making a fire burst in his lungs. Then instantly, and effortlessly, he could breathe.

Magnus Fin blinked over and over. His body felt warm and strong. That kiss had been like bellows to a fire. He was breathing underwater. And he could open his eyes and, in a blurry fashion, he could see. He stared at the strong white hand with smooth long fingers now holding his. Slowly his gaze traced the hand up the arm to the elbow, then further up to the shapely shoulder and finally to the face, the kind face of a woman.

"My name is Miranda," she said gently. "To greet you I have worn my human skin." Magnus Fin stared into her large green eyes. She looked human, beautiful and old in a wise, kind way. Long thick white hair tumbled down her back and reached to her knees. "We selkies do exist," she said, pressing Magnus Fin's hand, "we really do." The selkie woman looked into his eyes and smiled. "Now come and meet your kinsfolk," she said, and gently pulled her grandson through the sea. Then she stopped and looked at his feet, bound in trainers and making little headway in the water.

"Shoes are good for land, Magnus Fin," she said, "but you are part selkie. Webbed feet will serve you better. Take off your shoes, Fin. I'll take care of them."

So Magnus pulled off his trainers then stretched and wiggled his toes.

"Grand feet," said his grandmother, and for the first time Magnus felt proud of his feet. And she was right. It was easier to swim without his heavy shoes pulling him down.

Magnus Fin could see easily underwater now. Looking above him he could see the red rays of the setting sun stream through the water. Ahead of him the long snow-white hair of Miranda floated through the water, making him think suddenly about Mrs McLeod and Tarkin's seventeen words for snow. Good old Tarkin and his Alaskan mermaid. Then he thought about his father waving him off urgently and his mother handing him the moon-stone. When was that? Hours and minutes seemed to slip away in this dim watery world.

Magnus Fin let this beautiful snowy-haired sea maiden guide him. She wore a necklace of cowrie shells, a skirt of seaweed fronds and around her waist a belt of amber. As she swam her thick white hair billowed around her like a bridal gown. Magnus gaped in amazement as his grandmother guided him down through the ocean, parting waving seaweed fronds to take them through a dark kelp forest. Then on they swam through coral valleys where shoals of small darting fish brushed against his feet.

Magnus Fin shivered, especially when a pulsating pink jellyfish stretched out its long tentacles and tickled his face. "He's just curious!" Miranda laughed, but never slowed down for rest. She pointed to the ocean floor, carpeted with writhing brittle stars. Magnus Fin couldn't wait to tell Tarkin. But there was no time to stare. On and on they travelled, Miranda swimming and Magnus Fin being propelled through the water beside her, holding fast to her hand and kicking away for all he was worth. With his other hand he made round swimming gestures. Never had he swum so fast.

They had left the sun-filtered water behind and as they swam deeper the water darkened. Now, for the first time in his life, the blue pupils in his eyes did what they were made to do. They were like tiny strong torches that sent out beams of light through the dark water. Magnus Fin could see into caverns of swaying coral. He could see ghostly wrecks of fishing boats and sunken warships, some upside down, some broken in two. Here were rusting navies and rotting anchors

They swam over vast desert wastes of rippling sand. Magnus Fin stretched out his arm then recoiled quickly when he spotted a grotesque fish coming towards him. It was an anglerfish with its mouth gaping wide. Magnus tried to scream but only a bubbling noise sounded in the silent world. Miranda tugged him to safety and gently ruffled his wet black hair.

They could have been travelling like this for a long time or a short time when Miranda slowed her pace and gathered Magnus Fin into her arms. Ahead of them was a dark archway, hung limply with yellow seaweed.

"Through here," she said, lifting her slender arm and indicating towards the archway, "is where your father was born." Under the archway, like a barricade, was a rusty iron gate that looked as if it had been taken from a sunken ship. "We didn't always have a gate," she said sadly as she pushed the rusting bars aside. "Come, son of Ragnor, welcome to the Emerald Valley of the seal people, the home we call Sule Skerrie." The gate clunked behind them.

This floating dark world is where Dad is from? Magnus wondered, glancing around at the huge fronds of seaweed waving like dancers on either side of the cavern. The words of his father's song – *I'll see no more my Sule Skerrie* – haunted him. So he was here. In the place his father would see no more. His dear Sule Skerrie.

The thought that on land had seemed so unbelievable now seemed to him a fairly ordinary thought. Many boys visited the site of their father's birth. Magnus Fin was simply doing what many had done before him – the only difference was, this was under the sea.

The entrance to the cavern was decorated with mixed pickings from the wrecks of ships. On rocky ledges Magnus noticed china ornaments, computers, cooking pans, a glass chandelier, a brass candlestick, a ship's wheel, a wooden mermaid taken from the front of a boat and a dark green glass bottle. He stared at the bottle, a green glass bottle with a cork in it.

"Yes," said Miranda, noticing that Magnus Fin was staring at the odd collection of ornaments, especially the bottle. "We selkies love human things. And we love humans. Your father, after all, loves your mother."

Magnus Fin wanted to ask about the bottle. Was it his bottle? It looked like his bottle, but perhaps all dark green glass bottles look the same. But Miranda seemed to be in a hurry. She took the boy and guided him deeper into the cavern.

As they swam through the Emerald Valley, forests of green and red seaweed nodded to them and strings of shells rattled. Miranda paused then guided Magnus to a small cove.

"Here I will put on my seal skin," she said. "It is easier for us to travel that way underwater. I can swim much faster as a seal. When I change, son of Ragnor, know that I am still your grandmother, even though I will look different. To your eyes I will look like a seal, but look deep into my eyes and you will see the eyes of a selkie."

Magnus Fin stared as Miranda lifted up a pale fur and slipped into it, just like a human would slip into a coat. In seconds the fair-skinned woman had gone and now a cream speckled seal swam towards him. Fin trembled. He had never been so close to a seal before – then suddenly remembered that was not true. Only days, or was it weeks, ago he had been inches from a seal. But still he felt frightened. Suddenly he felt so alone.

He tried to scramble away but the seal swam towards him and looked deep into his eyes. It could no longer speak but the kind eyes seemed to impart many words. Fin relaxed, the trembling left him and the seal, nuzzling him, pushed him through the water with its nose. Now it was thoughts instead of speech that jumped from seal to boy, a strange kind of talking that sounded in Fin's head.

"Soon, Fin, you will meet your family. Come." The seal thought and Magnus Fin understood. He

was starting to get used to the idea of having a
seal for a grandmother. They swam deeper into the
cove and suddenly a young seal swam out of the
dark water and greeted them. The seal, in its own
way, embraced the human child, then, as though
on cue, a hundred seals swam from the shadowy
waters and surrounded Miranda and Magnus.

"Don't be afraid," Miranda said to him in her
thought-talk way, rubbing her head against the
boy's. "These are your kinsfolk."

Magnus Fin didn't know what he was supposed
to do. He lifted an arm through the water and
slowly waved to the seals, which were now grouped
around him, staring. They looked like gentle large
dogs with flippers instead of legs. Their eyes
seemed to see right into his heart. They didn't
wave back.

Maybe waving is not their custom, Magnus
thought. *They don't have arms like I do, just small
flippers*.

Then suddenly, as though reading Fin's thoughts,
they all started clapping their flippers and yelping
and singing. Magnus Fin's fears disappeared. He
grinned. Never had he heard such a joyous deep
trumpeting sound.

"Welcome," they seemed to be saying, "welcome,
son of Ragnor, welcome cousin, nephew, grandchild,
friend."

And while Magnus Fin stared, mesmerised by
this circle of seals swaying around him, they began
to dance. They swam over and under each other.
They did backflips. They somersaulted. They
flicked their tails and made the water bubble. They

sang until it sounded as though the wedding bells in some great watery cathedral were announcing the marriage of the century.

Magnus Fin cheered and clapped his hands, though that was a hard thing to do underwater as the heavy water slowed down every movement. In a curious way, even though he had two legs and two arms and no flippers, he felt at home. And here was his family. He wanted to hug them and get to know them. But suddenly the welcoming singing and yelping ceased and the dancing slowed into what looked to Magnus Fin like a funeral march.

The glad party mood had changed. Now the seals' cries were the saddest Magnus had ever heard, sadder even than his mother, sadder than a heron, sadder than a crow.

Magnus Fin felt his eyes fill up with tears. Just then his grandmother swam over to him and guided him to a chair made of scallop shells.

The crying seals grew quiet and swam aside to allow Miranda and Magnus Fin to pass. She rested herself in the great shell chair and brought her grandson to sit by her side. For a while Miranda was silent. Magnus gazed at the many green and yellow shining eyes of the seals that were gazing at him. It took him a while to see clearly but then he understood, every eye was weeping. This last song hadn't been some kind of strange welcome song; this was a lament.

Miranda lifted her flippers, and as she did so all the seals gathered around the great chair and folded their tails underneath them. They lay now in silence, like children at the feet of a storyteller.

Miranda was the one to tell the story, and whether she spoke or thought the words Magnus Fin couldn't tell.

"We have waited for you, son of Ragnor, for a very long time. Our celebrations for your third year were prepared. We were ready to meet you, to bless you, to initiate you into our world of water, but when you did not come we were worried. We swam beyond our realm looking for you. We put ourselves at risk searching for you. Ragnor promised he would bring you down to meet us. But Ragnor had been gone a long time. We thought perhaps he had lost his way. So your cousin Aquella, the brave and beautiful, said she would find you.

"Searching for you, she wandered into the realm of the false king – and he captured her." At the mention of this false king a pitiful moaning broke into the storyteller's tale. Magnus Fin shuddered at the name.

"Yes, Fin – a monster. We have known of him for many ocean years but never did we believe he could overcome the great Neptune. He was a giant squid, who feasted on whatever he could find in his deep dark place in the ocean. It seems he had a terrible appetite for man-made things. So he grew fat on human rubbish, on oil and plastic and toxic waste that would have killed most other creatures. But his body adapted to it, and grew ever stronger. His tentacles became enormous, sharp powerful and deadly. He grew more and more deformed – unrecognisable now as a squid: a mutant – huge, cruel and forever hungry."

A chilling silence fell. Magnus Fin didn't know the selkies never spoke of the false king. It filled them with terror – and grief – for this monster had kidnapped many beautiful young selkies.

Miranda nuzzled her grandson and carried on. "Yes, Fin, this monster captured your brave cousin. He robbed Aquella of her seal skin and kept her prisoner, to dance for him whenever he clicked his fingers and sing for him whenever he grew bored.

Then this false king, this nameless monster of the sea, sent his army of sharks to find us. *Were there more like Aquella?* he wanted to know. We were told that their master had never set his one eye upon any creature so lovely. You see, Fin, the false king has always desired to be human. He thought the selkie folk knew the secret of being human. The shark army came to find us and to tear off our seal skins. They found us, rounded up the young maidens and took them away."

Magnus Fin wrung his hands together, shivering at the thought of his own skin being ripped off. His grandmother stopped her sad tale for a moment and rubbed her nose gently across Magnus Fin's back, to comfort him. Then she carried on.

"That was eight years ago, Fin. Since then we have put up gates that we take from sunken ships, and we live here in fear. We don't know if our children are still alive and every day we cry for them. We haven't seen Aquella. We haven't seen our maidens. The false king has surely damaged their seal skins in his vain efforts to become human."

As Miranda spoke, the seal folk wept so much that Magnus Fin wondered whether that was why the sea was salty. After a pause his grandmother carried on with her story.

"The sharks captured twenty of our maidens and took them back to the monster's palace. Our bravest seal men went to King Neptune's cavern to enlist his help but by this time the false king had become too powerful. He had bullied all the sharks into joining his army. He threatened the lobsters with broken claws unless they became his police force, and he promised riches for the killer whales if they became his bodyguards. They were told they would feast like kings every night. And they do, Magnus Fin. They're eating the sea."

Magnus Fin saw one old walrus cry so much he looked as though he could never be consoled. The boy in his wetsuit, with his moon-stone dangling round his neck, held tight to his chair and breathed deeply. He too wanted to cry but sensed some adventure lay before him and, if he didn't feel brave he should at least try and look brave. The seals gazed at Magnus with hope, as though this small boy could put an end to their sorrows. Magnus Fin bit his lip and couldn't imagine what a lad like himself could possibly do to overcome monsters, killer whales, sharks and lobsters. Miranda's voice grew louder and more urgent.

"With the strongest creatures on the false king's side, Neptune was powerless to fight the monster. You will have heard of King Neptune?"

Fin nodded. Of course he'd heard of Neptune. His own room was named after him.

"Great King Neptune is the true king of the sea. He is good and strong and loves the ocean and the creatures in it. But, Fin, the monster's power has grown so terrible that even the mighty Neptune was forced to return to his cavern, where the sharks poisoned him then locked him up. They would have killed him. The monster and his army are powerful but, thank Neptune, not that powerful. Our king and all his loyal companions lie in his cavern in a deep sleep, and a terrible, noxious aura surrounds them, so that no sea creature can enter to waken them. And there he is to this day. King Neptune makes the waves and the waves bring freshness and life. His great work is not being done and so the sea is slowly dying."

Magnus Fin gulped. Miranda carried on. "With every new moon the sharks come to the gates demanding more and more maidens. We haven't let them in but it's only a matter of time. The gates are rusting. The locks are breaking. The next time they come I think the gates will burst open. Help us, son of Ragnor."

Magnus Fin stared at Miranda. Her eyes were closed now. He turned to look upon the circle of seal folk. Their many voices seemed to be begging, ringing, screeching, "Help us, son of Ragnor, help us."

His head clamoured with their chants. His heart kicked in his ribs. His eyelids drooped and his chin dropped to his chest. He felt so, so tired, but still the chanting went on, "Help us, son of Ragnor, help us!"

"I thought I came here to get my birthday gift," Magnus said. "I thought I'd get my hansel." But as he spoke the words, he felt how small and unimportant they seemed compared with the loss of the young selkies and the dying of the sea.

How selfish, he thought to himself, his eyelids closing and everything blurring, *and how tired I feel, how very, very ti—*

Chapter Fourteen

Ragnor spooned hot chocolate into his wife's favourite mug. He heaped in two spoonfuls of sugar and stirred it. As the hot chocolate made its own tiny whirlpool, his thoughts raced to his son and the whirlpool at the black rock. He glanced up at the kitchen clock. 10.23 pm. Ragnor blew on the hot chocolate, making creamy bubbles form on the surface, wishing with all his selkie heart that all would be well for Fin.

"This hot chocolate is taking for ever," Barbara called from her room, though it was Magnus Fin she really cared about, not the hot chocolate.

"Just a minute," Ragnor called, "you don't want to burn your lips." He blew again and his breath rippled over the thick brown liquid, making little crinkled waves.

The moon rose through the slit in the curtain so that Barbara could see it, full and silvery white. "I don't want to die of starvation," she called, and a tremble of worry shook her voice.

Ragnor entered the room and handed his wife the steaming mug. "The moon is full," said Ragnor, sitting on the edge of her bed. Then he stood up slowly, walked over to the window and opened the curtains. "Let's allow the night in," he said, flooding the room with silvery light. Barbara cupped her hands around the mug, stared at the moon, sipped her drink then looked across at her husband.

"That's good," she said, "and, Ragnor, I know I have said this before and perhaps I'll die saying it – but believe me – I am truly sorry for burning your seal skin."

"I know," said Ragnor, nodding his grey head, "I know."

"Here's to our son," she said gently, lifting the mug to her lips. Ragnor closed his eyes and echoed her words.

"Our son," he said, "our son."

Chapter Fifteen

Miranda let Magnus Fin sleep. With a wave of her hand the circle of seal-people twisted round, their tails swishing the water into bubbles, and swam swiftly away. While the boy slept, curled up at the foot of the scallop-shell chair with a stone on his lap to keep him down, Miranda gathered dulse and carrageen from her seaweed kitchen, collecting the tasty leaves in a deep-bottomed scallop shell. She mashed it with a stone, mixing it into a fine pulp. A strong smell drifted into Magnus Fin's slumber. The tang reminded him of the beach at low tide.

"Here, it'll give you strength," Miranda said, seeing Magnus Fin's eyes slowly open. She handed him a white china bowl full of the pungent-smelling soup. "The bowl I took from a sunken ship," she said, with laughter in her voice, "but the soup is my own."

"It wasn't the *Titanic*, was it?" he said, taking the bowl.

"Well now – all seas join up eventually – so it might have been ..."

"The *Titanic*!" said Magnus Fin, brightening up. "Wow! I've got a sign from the *Titanic*. It says 'Ballroom'."

"And when it is time for you to return," said his grandmother, "I will give you another sign. I have one that says 'Captain's Quarters'. That'll be a good hansel, eh?"

Fin nodded and his eyes grew wide. He became so excited about having another sign that he almost forgot the tale of woe he had been told. Was it yesterday? Everything seemed like a dream.

As he brought the spoon to his mouth he thought, *But if this is a dream, it's going on for a very long time*. He recalled he had never eaten in a dream before and although the soup smelled horrible he took it and drank it. He could feel the strong seaweed taste on his tongue. He felt the soup going down his throat. As he swallowed strength seeped into him. If this was a dream – it was vivid. But it must be a dream; never in real life would he eat soup as disgusting as that.

"Come now," said Miranda, putting the empty bowl and the stay-down stone aside and guiding the boy up. "We have work to do." She picked up a small sponge called "mermaid's purse" and took something out of it, then with her other hand she pulled her grandson through the water. As before, she swam behind and propelled him through the water with her nose. They journeyed back through the caverns of the seal people, back along the Emerald Valley they had travelled down – when? Was it only yesterday?

Magnus Fin peered into fantastical chambers with whorled shells the size of footballs decorating the floors. Down alleyways he saw shoals of fish darting over swaying pink sea anemones, rainbow trout and salmon, silver eels and flat fish. From rocky shadows and dim waters seal women and men peered. When they reached the old iron gate Magnus could feel Miranda's flipper push against his hand.

"We are venturing beyond our realm now," she said as she unlocked the great iron lock and pushed the iron bars aside. "If you feel fear, grasp the moon-stone you have around your neck. It will help you. You are going to need great strength, Fin."

Magnus had forgotten about his birthday stone, dangling now on a lace around his neck. This seal woman guiding him through the sea was his father's mother. He said it to himself several times. Sometimes the idea sounded ridiculous and sometimes it felt completely normal.

Magnus Fin reached up to touch the stone and as he did he felt his father near him. "Be strong," he was saying. "Be brave, my son." So it was true. The door at low tide was real. He, Magnus Fin, was half human and half selkie. This journey was no dream.

As though divining his thoughts, Miranda nuzzled his back tenderly. As they travelled, she told her grandson more of her story.

"Don't you notice how still everything is down here? Haven't you asked yourself where the mighty waves are, the surging sea? Can't you smell stagnation in the water?"

With each question some slumbering sense in Magnus Fin awoke. He recalled his father telling him that the sea was dying, and that his teacher, Mrs Mcleod, had said the same thing. Yes, it *was* eerily still, there was a whiff of decay, even the fronds of seaweed seemed to sway in a forlorn motion, and the dogfish lazing on the ocean bed looked listless. Magnus had simply assumed that's how it was deep under the sea – dank, dark and dreary. Miranda read his thoughts, or was it that Magnus Fin spoke aloud? He wasn't sure any more.

"Ah, Fin, you think this dull murky green-grey is the true shade of our world? You think this stench of slow rotting is the true scent of the sea? Son of Ragnor, I hope with all my selkie heart you will see our world in its true flashing and vibrant colours. Before Neptune fell asleep, every pounding wave and crashing breaker was like a shower for us. Great waves would sway our world with blues, greens, translucent emeralds, turquoise, shimmering silver and sparkling gold. The sun filtered a rainbow down through the ocean and everything was so clean and fresh. But now King Neptune does not thrash the deep. If he does not waken soon the sea as we know it will die."

Questions bumped themselves up against Magnus Fin's brain like dodgem cars. Some of them tumbled out: "But why? Why did the false king win? Why was Neptune not strong enough to fight back? It's not our fault, is it? We're going to clean the beach soon. Mrs McLeod says that will help."

Miranda sent her thoughts back to her grandson while all the time they journeyed on: "It is good to ask why, Fin, and often I have asked the same thing. Why is the false king so powerful? How did he trick the great King Neptune? I have come up with one word. It is the only word that makes sense. Fear. We under the sea are no more puppets than you are on land. It seems we, like you, have a choice – love or fear. Many are afraid, Fin, so many. The sharks are afraid, the lobsters are afraid, yes, even the false king is afraid. You, Magnus Fin? Are you afraid?"

Magnus Fin gulped and felt his heart kick in his ribs. The very mention of monsters made him almost faint. He had felt afraid when Tarkin had gone on so easily about the Loch Ness Monster. He nodded his head. He couldn't pretend he was brave when he wasn't.

"Then grasp your moon-stone, Fin, and the fear will leave you."

Magnus took hold of his precious stone, and as he did he felt the fear melt away, like snow in the warm sun.

On they journeyed, through dark valleys choked with weeds and sunken ships, through vast deserts of sand and skeletons, between long dim crevices where plastic bottles, car parts, first-aid kits and broken bicycles floated around like ghosts. If it was not for his torch-like eyes, Magnus Fin wouldn't have seen a thing. His eyes lit up the dim, eerie wreck of a submarine, covered in barnacles and seaweed. Magnus wanted to dive deeper and examine it, but Miranda was in a hurry and in moments the ghostly submarine was far behind them. Miranda pushed on through the water. Boats lay smashed in their final harbour. Magnus Fin thought of the treasures that must surely be stacked up in the holds of these sunken ships. He wanted to explore. But they swam on, on and on.

They rarely met a fish or living creature now, though sometimes Magnus Fin heard deep bellowing sounds. "It's the call of the false king's bodyguards, the killer whales," said Miranda. "Their terrifying bellow reaches hundreds of miles through the water."

Miranda slowed down. "Don't worry, Fin, they are far from here." But turning from her grandson she looked anxiously around her. She hoped the monster's army was far away – but suddenly she felt tremors in the sea. The smooth water rocked. Miranda sniffed the stench of the monster's army. She could hear way up in the distance a crashing, smashing noise. Quickly she grasped Fin's arm and propelled him up towards the surface.

"Fin, I hear the false king's army. They are wrecking boats again. It is sport for them. Quick – we might be able to save some poor people from drowning. Oh, Fin – your strength is already to be tested."

Miranda the seal swam now like a lightning streak, with Magnus Fin wrapping his small arms around her tail and clinging on for dear life. In no time they had arrived close to the sea's surface. Disturbed, the killer whales, thankfully, had gone. Magnus saw a rosy glow dapple the water's surface above him. Then suddenly, breaking the smooth surface, he saw bodies drop down through the water, their arms thrashing, their legs kicking, their faces distorted with drowning.

"Go, Fin! Use every ounce of strength you have. Push them back up to the surface. Quick!"

Miranda left him. She swam towards the man who was falling the deepest. She pressed her head under him and propelled him upwards.

Magnus Fin panicked. *What*, he thought desperately, *could he do?* He saw a young boy float towards him, his face all puffed up, his arms thrashing out ahead of him. Without thinking, Magnus reached out, grabbed the boy by his t-shirt then swam upwards with all his strength to return him to the air. The boy thrashed his arms so much that he hit Magnus across the face, but still Magnus held him tight. He brought him to the surface where he heard the boy gasp loudly. Magnus Fin left him there, clutching a spar of the shattered hull, and dived back under the sea. There was no time to lose.

Another boy, a bigger one, was sinking fast through the water. Magnus dived down to him then pulled at his heavy jacket and dragged him upwards. This boy was heavy, much heavier than the other boy, and much heavier than Magnus. He struggled to make any headway. He felt his arms weaken. He wanted to let go. He couldn't lift any more. He wanted to scream from the pain in his arms. He wanted to drop this drowning boy.

But then he saw into the boy's panicked, staring eyes and remembered how he had pulled Tarkin from the water. Tarkin! Tarkin who said he'd be chanting for him. *I hope you are chanting now, Tarkin*, Fin thought, his arms in agony but determined now to hold on. With an almighty effort he dragged the boy up. The surface was close now. The light rays were streaming through the water. With a last huge heave Fin hoisted the boy to the surface.

In seconds Miranda was by his side. "Good. If it is not their time to die they will survive. Come, Fin, we must go." And again Magnus clasped her tail and they dived deep down under the sea.

"You were strong, Magnus Fin," he heard her say. "You'll need more of that for what lies ahead. Soon we will reach King Neptune's cavern. Waken him, Fin. You are half human. Do you understand? So much strength from the land you bring down to our watery world. I would not survive. Even now as we approach I feel my strength sap away. Here, Fin, take this salmon bone – the key to the cavern. Please, son of Ragnor, waken Neptune, and help us fight the false king."

Magnus Fin felt his grandmother push a small bone into the palm of his hand. He grasped it, looking as he did at Miranda. She seemed older and slower. Her voice was growing fainter.

"We have no time to waste, Fin. Hold the bone tight and let's go on."

Chapter Sixteen

For a long time Miranda and Magnus Fin swam. Time itself had little meaning under the water. Magnus Fin didn't know if he had been underwater for hours or weeks. He didn't know if he had travelled through this dark stinking water for a short distance or for hundreds of miles. He hoped the boys they had dragged to the surface had made it safely home to the land – but even that thrashing and kicking and heaving seemed to have happened a long time ago.

Finally Miranda spread her flippers and circled her body round to slow down. Now Magnus Fin had a chance to look around. His penetrating blue eyes shone through the murky water to land upon a huge cavernous rock, hung with thick plankton and shells.

"We have arrived," Miranda said, her voice a faint whisper, her body old and tired looking. "This is King Neptune's cavern."

"Like my room," he said, and for a moment the memory of his fishing net and shells, his box of treasures and bones, flashed through his mind, but like a vague dream from long ago. Gazing through the hazy water he saw that this beautiful cavern, decked with coral, pearls and shells, was far, far greater than his own simple Neptune's Cave. This

cavern on the ocean bed had a rock for a door. A
million shells decorated the entranceway. It should
have been splendid but an eerie stillness and thick
green hue gave Neptune's cavern a ghostly feeling.
A shiver ran the length of Magnus Fin's spine.

"We have come a long way, Fin, and a deep way,"
his grandmother said, breaking in on his thoughts.
And suddenly Fin understood she was going to
leave him. Already she was swimming away from
him. She was going to leave him in this strange
place all alone.

"Some things, Fin, have to be done alone." She
propelled herself backwards, summoning up every
last ounce of strength to stop herself falling under
the spell of sleep. "If I entered this place I would
fall asleep immediately. Look into my eyes, Fin.
See how weak I have become."

Fin saw and a great pity welled up in him. He
wanted to go with her.

"You, with your human strength, have the power
to stay awake. You are living between the worlds,
Magnus Fin – you have a chance to heal the sea.
And you proved your strength when you found the
courage to rescue the drowning boys. Now this test
must be faced alone. I have brought you this far. I
must go. Later I will return, Fin. Go now. Please
wake Neptune. Please, son of Ragnor, bring back
the waves."

"But how – stop!" shouted Magnus Fin. "What
am I supposed to do?" He tried to reach for his
grandmother but already she was gone.

Magnus Fin was alone, a salmon bone in his small
hand and the great rock of Neptune before him.

Chapter Seventeen

Mrs McLeod was in her kitchen making a late-night cup of tea. The schoolteacher's house stood at the top of the village, and from the kitchen window she had a great view down to the sea. She hardly noticed the kettle had boiled; she was so busy staring out at the silver pathway the full moon made over the ocean and the red pathway made by the setting sun.

"Might there be such a thing as a biscuit?" said her husband, popping his head round the kitchen door. "Full moon always brings on the munchies. Not to mention that this hard-working fisherman has been out at sea all day. I'm starving."

Mrs McLeod laughed then plonked a whole packet of caramel wafers on a plate. "I was miles away," she said, "imagining a world under the sea. Must be these children of mine with their wild imaginations. Ha! They'll have me believing in mermaids next!"

Mrs McLeod brought the tea things through to the sitting room and sank down on the sofa with a sigh, and then a yawn, and then a little shiver up her spine.

"Johnny," she said, looking across at her husband who was busy dunking a biscuit into his tea, "that moon out there does something funny to me. Gives me the heebie-jeebies, so it does. Looks like the moon is right in this room. Looks like the moon is sitting right on my biscuit."

She bit into her caramel wafer then sighed again. "You know we've got this new boy in the school?" she went on, cupping her hands around her teacup. "Comes from America. Tarkin he's called. How's that for a name? Remember I told you about him? Earrings and all that. Well, he said he saw a mermaid. Really. Thing is, he told it as though it was true. Had the whole class so quiet you could have heard a pin drop. Made me all shivery. I didn't know what to say."

"That's not like you, Carol."

"I know. He's a strange one. First that Magnus Fin. I mean, he's strange enough – always picking bones and stuff off the beach and standing on his own at breaktimes, not to mention his eyes. Now I've got an American called Tarkin to cope with who, I kid you not, wears two earrings, a necklace, believes in mermaids and has become a great pal of our Magnus Fin. Other boys their age talk about football and Nintendos. Not them, they talk about mermaids. They're just not normal somehow."

"Better than them all looking the same, thinking the same, doing exactly the same thing. I like Tarkin. Never met him of course, but from what you've told me, Carol, I like him. Magnus Fin's not bad either." Johnny bit off another corner of his biscuit and ate it, making little satisfying noises as he did so.

"Um … Johnny?" his wife said.

"Aye, Carol. Fire away. What is it?"

"See when you're out in the boat. You know …

did you, I mean, have you … um, did you ever see a mermaid?" Carol McLeod sat up straight. The full moon shone on her lap.

"A mermaid? No," he said, "not yet anyway. But I've seen many a selkie. Aye, I've seen them. Many times. Oh, Carol, I could tell you some stories."

Carol didn't know what to say. She coughed. She spluttered. "Really?"

"I certainly could. I didn't think you were interested but I'd love to tell you a story from the sea."

Carol McLeod looked at her husband, then, not quite sure what she was letting herself in for, nodded, sat back and made herself comfortable with the full moon on her lap.

"Well, Carol, once upon a time," said Johnny, "far out in the cold North Sea, there lived a selkie …"

Chapter Eighteen

Magnus Fin stared at the great rock barring the entrance to Neptune's cavern. With his torch-light pupils he could make out, through the dark water, massive swaying fronds of seaweed. The cavern seemed to be shaped like a great conch shell. Through the dimness he could see that some of the cavern was made of an orange stone. Miranda told him it was amber. She was swimming away from him but still her thoughts called to him.

"I must leave you here, Fin. We ocean dwellers have tried all we can; it is said only a human who can live under the sea can now open the door to Neptune's cavern. You know both worlds, Magnus Fin. Your mother was born on the land. You are our only hope. I must return to our valley; it is not safe for me here. Remember the stone around your neck, son of Ragnor. If you come into danger it will give you strength. Goodbye, Magnus Fin."

By now Magnus had floated up to the great rock, and though his heart was thumping he searched for a hole in the rock, for a place to insert his bone key. He felt for the place, his hand frantically patting the rough surface of the rock door. "I can't find a keyhole!" he shouted in his thoughts as his grandmother swam away from him.

"It is there," she called out, "in the middle ..." but her thoughts were too faint now to make out any more.

Magnus Fin had never felt so desolate in his whole life. Around him was nothing but hundreds of miles of dark water. For a moment he felt an almighty fear rise up from the soles of his feet as though it would swallow him completely. Magnus grasped his moon-stone and the fear subsided. Still the boy floated alone, treading water under the sea, until the overpowering fear was gone.

Braver now, he turned around and banged with his fist on the great rock door of Neptune's cavern. The bone was so tiny, the door so huge. Never would he find the keyhole. He heard his knock reverberate within the cavern, growing louder and louder each time. To his ears the knocking sounded like thunder, but no one or nothing answered. Now he thumped louder and called out, "NEPTUNE!" Still no one came. No one heard him. His heart gave a leap. In the middle of the mighty door, suddenly, he spied a tiny keyhole.

Magnus Fin peered through the keyhole with his green eye and saw, inside the great hallway, a thousand creatures of the deep – all of them sound asleep. Some were floating, some curled up on the watery floor. There were salmon and herring, eels, crabs, seals and dolphins, porpoises and lobsters – all of them floating in sleep.

Magnus Fin's heart was pounding so loudly now, he thought it might wake Neptune. He fumbled with the salmon bone. He tried to pull it up through the water. His eyelids drooped. He felt an overwhelming urge to sleep. He recalled Miranda's pleas and fumbled with the bone. Although the bone was tiny it seemed, suddenly, to weigh a ton. It took every ounce of strength to drag it up through the water towards the keyhole.

The effort was sapping him. More than anything he wanted to lie down and sleep. Why, he wondered, did his grandmother leave him? And where had she gone? And why did he have to do this alone? He was only eleven, wasn't he? He was still a child. As he heaved at the bone, now with two hands, he recalled his father's words: he was both child and man now – or neither child nor man – he was between worlds, and this thing he would have to do alone. He had come this far. He was at the gates of the great King Neptune's cavern and he couldn't even manage to put a key into a keyhole. He could save boys from drowning but he couldn't open a door. Whatever task he had to do it seemed he had failed already.

"Help!" he shouted, turning round frantically, circling his arms through the water and searching for Miranda. But even with his torch-light eyes beaming through the murky sea, Miranda was nowhere to be seen.

"Help me!" he called again, not wanting this adventure any more, feeling too young, too lonely, too weak. He couldn't lift the bone up to the keyhole. He wasn't strong enough. If it was a dream he wanted to wake up.

"Help!" he shouted, tears now stinging his eyes. But no one came. Magnus Fin banged frantically on the cavern door, over and over. It rattled. It shook. But no amount of banging could wake the sleeping creatures inside.

Exhausted, his little fist uncurled. The salmon bone floated down through the dim water. Magnus Fin's head nodded, his eyelids felt so heavy. A great weariness stole over him, as though he had suddenly been pierced by an arrow of sleep. Magnus Fin slumped down at the gates to Neptune's cavern, closed his eyes, and slept.

Chapter Nineteen

When Magnus Fin awoke, he found himself face to face with a sharp-toothed great white shark.

"Was the little boy dreaming then?" said the shark, curling his wide lips and smiling horribly. "Hmmm? Was the little wee boy with the little two legs having a little kip then? Hmmm?"

Magnus Fin wriggled backwards, staring at the glinting-eyed lisping creature, who moved closer. The shark's razor-sharp teeth flashed. Magnus edged back further, but the creature came even closer till Magnus felt the back of his head press against Neptune's door. The terrible creature was inches away and edging nearer – as though he'd eat the boy up in one quick bite. Miranda had said he should hold the moon-stone, but the shark had pressed its body against Magnus Fin's hands.

"Oh? Little human boy got little handies too? Oooh? So teeny-weeny. Hmm? Handies and feeties? Hmm? Trying to open the door, was you? Hmm? Neptune still fast asleep then? Silly Neptune. The little boy lost the little key then? Hmm? Stupid little human boy."

If this was a nightmare it had gone on long enough. Magnus Fin wanted to shout out, to call for his dad, but no sound came. He opened his mouth like a fish underwater, but could not speak.

Horrified, he watched the menacing shark dart down to the seabed, flick up the floating salmon bone with its snout, catch it between its sharp teeth and swallow it.

"Mm! Nice," he said, smacking together his terrible jaws. Then, changing his tone, he mocked, "Daddy's not here." The ugly creature lisped and hissed like a snake. Quick as lightning the shark wound its tail fast around the boy's legs and hauled him up. "You're coming with me, little two legs. You're coming to a really big palace. The king will like you."

Magnus Fin grabbed at the tail and tried to wrench it off his legs, but it was clamped fast around him as hard as iron.

Now the shark flicked his tail from side to side, hurtling the boy back and forth through the water. "Splish-splash," jeered the shark as though this was some kind of funfair ride. "Oooh, splishie-splash!"

Then the shark took off, speeding through the dark water with his prisoner locked in a tail wrench behind him. The shark swam much faster than Miranda had done. Even with his captive wriggling and squirming in the hold of his tail, the shark ploughed menacingly through the murky waters at great speed.

"Home sweet home," said the shark at last. "Now you'll see a real king." His horrible babyish lisp had gone. He uncurled his tail and hurtled Magnus Fin through the water. The boy landed on a jagged stone and would have hurt himself badly had the water not slowed him down.

"Meet his most powerful majesty – the king."
The sugary, babyish speech was now hard and
cutting. With his tail the shark flicked open the
massive gold-studded gates that stood in front of
the place where the boy was now lying.

Magnus Fin looked up in a daze. This palace
was far bigger than Neptune's cavern. The front
wall was so huge Magnus Fin couldn't see the top
of it. The palace gates were so wide Magnus Fin
couldn't see an end to them. The shark's tail spun
out and flicked the boy inside the gates, as if it was
a cricket bat and Magnus was a ball. He bounced
over the threshold in slow watery motion.

Magnus Fin landed in the corner of a vast
room studded all round with sharp jewels. From
doorways and corridors, tiger sharks, eels, skates,
killer whales and lobsters patrolled. All eyed the
human child with curiosity and suspicion.

As Magnus Fin lay with the back of his head
pressed against a ruby he heard a massive yawn
shudder through the palace. Magnus watched,
terrified, as the heads of every creature turned
swiftly in the direction of the mighty yawn. The
gargantuan groaning yawn came again. A sound
like thunder echoed through the palace. It –
whatever it was – was coming closer. The ground
that Magnus lay upon quaked. He clutched at
his moon-stone and though it couldn't take away
the fear completely it gave him some feeling of
strength.

Thousands of crabs scuttled frantically over the
floor, first to the left, then to the right, sweeping,
dusting, polishing, scrubbing, anxious to appear

busy. Magnus Fin lay slumped in the great hallway, shaking till he thought his teeth would crumble.

The palace walls shook with the vibration of the groan. The lobsters shuddered. The crabs quaked. The sharks shivered. The killer whales glided forward menacingly like submarines, their white eye-patches glowing. The king was coming in their trail.

Magnus Fin breathed deeply in the new way he now had of breathing, the underwater way. Still clutching the stone his father had given him, the blinding numbing fear left him, and in its place came a feeling of strength and curiosity for what would happen next.

He thought of his father. Would he be in his cave with the wood smoke drifting over the water? He thought of his mother, in bed, afraid to show her haggard face. He thought of the seal people and the sound of their singing and weeping. He thought of all the sleeping fish he had seen in Neptune's cavern. He thought of Miranda. This was no dream – he knew that now. Which meant the beautiful Miranda *was* his grandmother, and though she had gone he was sure she would be back. He felt a warm courage fill his heart.

The monster groaned again.

Chapter Twenty

The cold-eyed tiger sharks, the monster's army, bowed low. A pod of killer whales, the monster's bodyguards, patrolled the hallway, their paddle-shaped flippers clearing the way. The lobsters, the monster's police force, stood to attention on either side of the grand room. The eels, the monster's servants, hovered at the ready. Magnus Fin slunk back into the shadows, hoping he would be overlooked amongst such powerful armies and frenzied activity.

From his ruby corner, bumped up against the wall, Magnus Fin looked on in horror as the front of the monster king came into view. A long thin luminous green tongue darted through the dark water. The tongue protruded from a narrow stretched mouth that pulled at the black and hideous face of the monster. The tongue was like an eel, the face like a giant's squashed football, but uglier. The monster had only one eye that pulsed horrifically in the centre of his face. An eye more awful, so bulging, red-veined, pulsing and quivering, would be hard to imagine. If there was anything pleasing to look at, regarding the monster's head, it was his crown. Many necklaces had been tied together to make a jewelled band, which the false king wore around his head. Behind the pulled slimy head the monster had a long scaly snake-like body, and behind the trunk of this body, Magnus Fin could now see, flicked several enormous tentacles. Like metallic blades they whipped dangerously from side to side, stirring up the dark stinking water to a froth and killing whatever got in their way.

The monster's entrance was heralded with a loud blowing of trumpets, a clashing of cymbals and a great deal of cheering and bowing – and on account of the lashing tentacles, a great deal of killing too. Magnus Fin did not bow but stared at this terrible creature. He saw, as more of him came into view, that draped around his long pulsing body were hundreds of plastic-bottle belts or necklaces – except the monster had no neck. And around his awful tentacles he wore bracelets made of tin cans and junk. One of his trinkets looked like a fridge.

Magnus Fin felt sick. This awful sight was far worse than he had imagined when Miranda had told her tale. She had told him the monster wanted to be human. So here he was dressed in all the rubbish that had once belonged to humans. Magnus Fin pushed himself further back into the shadows and kept a grasp of his moon-stone. Though the entrance hall to the king's palace was bigger than a football stadium, the monster and his thrashing junk-adorned tentacles only just fitted in. In comparison, Magnus Fin was tiny, hardly bigger than the vile monster's one yellow tooth.

Magnus pressed himself still further back, desperately hoping everyone had forgotten about him. But then, with dread sinking into his tummy, he saw that every creature had now turned to look at him. The very reason for the monster's arrival was to see the two-legged prisoner – the boy who could breathe underwater.

"Where's the human?" a voice like the grating of metal bellowed out and the water shook. The one pulsing eye, quivering like a jellyfish, scanned the room. It wobbled as it searched back and forth like a periscope. It seemed to pant. Suddenly the jelly-red eye fixed on the small crumpled shadow in the corner.

"HEH–EH!" the monster cried. The eye had found Magnus Fin. Instantly the long green tongue flicked out, wound itself around Magnus Fin's legs and yanked him up close to the horrible one red eye.

Had Magnus not been holding tight to his moonstone, he would have died of fright. Magnus Fin stared at the monster, thinking as he did so that he had never set eyes on anything so hideous.

The monster stared back, his eye pulsing out and in, his tentacles razoring excitedly from side to side, killing whatever chanced to get in his way, which happened to be hundreds of crabs all busy cleaning.

The monster wobbled his head around as if showing off his crown. Then he attempted a smile, grimaced instead, and exposed one sharp yellow tooth and a horrible stench. "You admire my crown?" he hissed, drawing the boy even closer in the tongue-vice grip in which he held him captive.

"Um – yes, nice crown, but – ouch!" said Magnus Fin, staring into the red eye as he squirmed around. "You're hurting me. Can you let my legs go and control your tails? You are killing the crabs."

The monster had never, ever been spoken to in such a way. He found it amusing. Instantly he obeyed. Now he unwound his tongue and let Magnus Fin float about in front of him. The monster was fascinated by his two-legged prisoner. He watched the two tiny legs tread water and the two thin arms make circles.

The boy was unaware of the huge advantage he had over the monster. Magnus Fin had what the monster so dearly desired. He had two legs, two arms, a human heart and a human brain. He could breathe on the land, and under the water.

The monster tried to copy Magnus, but he had no arms, and when he tried to tread water with his tentacles he killed a few more hundred crabs. Seeing the poor creatures smashed as though they were no more than toys in the hands of an angry child, Magnus Fin felt his heart burst.

"That's cruel!" shouted Magnus Fin. "How could you? Stop it."

"That's cruel – how could you? Stop it? Oh! Heh-heh-heh, oh, how sweet," said the monster, trying to talk just like Magnus Fin, but his voice sounding no more human than the sound of a knife scratched on a blackboard.

"Feed the human," commanded the monster. "Look after him." Immediately the lobsters surrounded Magnus Fin, and with their pincers hooked into various parts of his wetsuit, they

swiftly transported him to another room. The
eels swam ahead pushing doors open. Every room
seemed to be massive. As they glided through the
palace, the boy gazed at the lavish jewels lining
every wall.

"Yes, opals and rubies and gold, very nice, eh?"
said one of his transporters, the red lobster nearest
to Magnus Fin's face. "His most great majesty is
very fond of treasure."

Magnus could only nod to the informative lobster
before he was taken in to a banqueting hall and
pushed down before an enormous table. Pressing
him on to the chair, the lobster clamped its pincer
across the boy's arm, like a policeman's handcuff.

"Ouch!" Magnus Fin yelled.

"Oops! Sorry," said the lobster, opening its
pincer, "I'm not used to weak human flesh."

Magnus Fin rubbed his arm, thankful for his
thick rubber wetsuit.

"Well, you'd better eat then," the lobster said,
and Magnus Fin stared at the mountain of food.
The table, the upturned hull of a sunken ship, was
so loaded with food it sunk in the middle. Magnus
Fin, with the fear gone, found he was starving. He
feasted, sucking oysters and mussels from their
shells, while wrapping his feet around the chair to
keep himself down.

As he ate, a sweet ringing music filled the hall.
Magnus Fin gazed around him. In the murky
water he could see nothing at first, but gradually
his pupils penetrated the dark. A beam of eye-
light fell upon a girl. She was seated on a rock in
an alcove of the room singing a mournful song.

Looking around him, Magnus Fin could see more and still more girls with moon-white skin and long black hair, each one more beautiful than the one before, and each one seated in an alcove behind bars. Some of them played harps. Some played silver flutes. Some blew softly into conch shells. One in particular, with deep sad black eyes and black hair trailing down her back, sang softly and stared at Magnus. She reminded him of someone, but he wasn't sure who.

With a sickening feeling in the pit of his stomach, Magnus Fin suddenly realised – these were the selkies, and they were all prisoners of the false king. Somewhere here was his cousin Aquella, the girl who had set out to try and find him when he was three years old.

Magnus Fin wanted to call out to them, to tell them that he was Magnus Fin, son of Ragnor, grandson of Miranda, but as soon as Magnus opened his mouth to speak, his small voice was swallowed by the groan of the monster.

The bulging red eye, the flicking green tongue, the stretched black face, all came groaning and smiling horribly into the banqueting hall. The selkies ceased their music. The monster drew his neck and head up to the table, where it crashed down with a thud, making the food still left there jump up into the water and float around. The monster peered at the boy with his shuddering eye.

"You are my guest," he said, his wide mouth gaping up and down with each word. "Teach me to be like you, human."

Magnus Fin leant his chin on his hand so he could hold his moon-stone undetected. The monster tried to copy the boy and brought one of his awful tentacles up to rest under his mouth. But the monster couldn't sit like the boy. Every time he tried he failed, and with each failure he grew more and more irritated.

"I am the greatest king that ever lived under the sea. I'd be a billionaire on the land with my magnificent treasure chest. I am the most powerful, the most feared, but I am bored with the sea. It's dark down here. It stinks. And there's no one interesting to talk to. But I have seen your sunken ships. I have seen your great cruise liners, your oilrigs. Lots I brought down. One whip of my tentacles and bang – crash – down they come. I have seen what wonders you have on the land, what riches you possess, what magnificent buildings you have. I want to rule the land. Yes, I want to be king there too. It will be fun, more fun than here. I need to breathe in air, that's all. I need to know your secret, you tiny two-legged thing. That's why you're still alive. I've tried before, you know. I've brought down sea captains, sailors, fishermen, swimmers, surfers; I've pulled them all under. It's so easy. But they all died, so quickly, every stupid one. Only you, tiny thing, have stayed alive. So you see, human child, you are my teacher."

With the terrible monster so close, Magnus Fin was now quaking like a leaf. The stench of the monster's breath was like a sewer. Magnus could only stop from fainting by keeping one eye on the sad and gentle-eyed maiden in the alcove. Magnus couldn't think of anything to say. He scratched at his face.

In a flash one of the awful tentacles of the monster curled up. In horror Magnus Fin saw that the monster was trying to scratch his own face – and failing miserably.

"Too bad!" he screamed, almost deafening Magnus. "I know you humans have machines for everything, so who needs hands?" Suddenly the monster stopped talking and stared at Magnus Fin's eyes. It felt unnerving having one eye stare at two eyes. Especially when that one eye was the most hideous pulsing bloodshot thing you could imagine.

"Of course," roared the monster. "Heh! I get it! It's your eyes, isn't it? That's it, heh-heh, I've got it. One eye for this world and one for the dry world: that world up there, where you have great buildings, huge palaces, cars, aeroplanes, everything! Heh! I'm a genius. I've worked it out. I might not have stupid little hands but I have a brain. You thought you'd keep it from me. You didn't know I was so clever, eh?"

The tentacles swished through the water. Magnus Fin squirmed in his seat and felt sick. "I'll take your eyes," hissed the monster. Coming so menacingly close, the boy could smell greed in his stinking hot breath. "Being blind won't be too bad. It's so dark and boring down here anyway; there isn't much to see. And you'll still have your little ears. I'll leave my girls down here to sing for you and you can keep your little legs and your little arms. These girls, they aren't really human.

Not really. I thought they were. They tricked me. They are seals and I have got their dirty little seal skins. But you – you are a human. I know it. I can smell it. Now I, king of the sea, command you: give me your eyes!"

Magnus Fin kept hold of his moon-stone. "Free the seal women first," he blurted out. The monster laughed – a horrid thin high laugh. Magnus Fin blinked. He thought of the monster ripping out his two eyes. Though the thought filled him with horror, he managed to face the monster and remain calm. "Set them all free," he said again, "and give them their skins."

"Oh, all right, all right," replied the monster huffily. "Who wants half-humans when I can have it all? I was going to marry one of them but I couldn't make up my mind, so I kept them all, even though their mournful songs were getting on my nerves. I thought I could be like them and find my way on to the land but, heh-heh, their silly little furs wouldn't fit me."

Magnus Fin stared at the hideous creature, trying not to show the horror he felt. "We," continued the false king, "you could say, had to damage a skin, but it was all in the name of science – heh-heh! If my little human says they must be released then it will be so. But it means you will have no music when I leave you behind. Nothing to hear, nothing to see. It will be very boring. But if you insist – guards!" he bellowed, shaking up the murky waters. Ten hammerhead sharks appeared, looking ready to tear the flesh from the human's bones. "Free the seal girls," commanded the king, "and give them their skins – at least the skins we still have."

"Are you absolutely sure, your gracious majesty?" said one of the sharks who knew how much the monster enjoyed his singing girls.

"Are you daring to question your gracious majesty of the deep? Are you?" the false king bellowed. "Their stupid songs bore me – weepy stuff that's been annoying me for ages. Go on! Get on with it." The din was deafening.

"Well, if your gracious most reverent majesty is sick of the girls, how about us hammerheads having them?" said the shark, bowing to kiss the monster's tentacles. "We like a bit of a song to send us to sleep."

"You cheeky, ungrateful, ugly, good-for-nothing idiot! If I am not going to have my little singing girls, you're certainly not going to have them. One more bit of cheek from you and I'll pull your teeth out. Understand?"

"Not my teeth. Please, your majesty, not my teeth. I'll do it. Of course I'll do it! I'll set them free right away. Your most royal highness magnificent king," said the shark, whimpering and trying to kiss the king's tentacles.

"Oi! Get back here. Unlock the cages and you can forget about your slobbering kisses. In fact you can forget my tentacles all together. Gone, gone, gone. Soon they will be gone – and good riddance. I'm sick of them. Soon I'll get two legs and you'll kiss them and then I'll be out of here. Heh-heh-heh!"

The sharks bared their teeth, and with them they finally tore the cages and opened the rusty

doors of the alcoves. The girls in the cages stared
in fear and wonder. They dropped their harps,
dropped their flutes and slowly, when they saw the
sharks were not about to eat them, stretched their
arms out into the water.

"And don't forget their seal skins," shouted
young Magnus Fin, trying to make his tiny voice
sound powerful and commanding.

The monster swung his head round and fixed his
one eye on his prisoner. "I've changed my mind.
I'll keep the skins for my fur coat. I'll need one to
wear in the big city in the winter when it snows. I
might catch a cold." Then the creature laughed his
terrible laugh.

Magnus Fin saw the girls huddle together now
in a corner of the great room. A part of him didn't
want them to go. Then he would feel more alone
than ever. But he could almost hear their voices
begging for their skins. He repeated his command.

"You'll be able to get another coat," Magnus
said. "Give them back their seal skins."

"Oh, all right then," said the monster. "If you
insist, spoilsport. Lobsters, unlock the fur cage
and throw the skins out. I'll get a better coat. Go
on, get on with it. What are you gawking at?"

The lobsters were gawking because never in
their petrified lives had they seen anyone dare give
orders to their king. Frantically they scurried to
the great chamber where a mountain of seal skins
was piled up.

As soon as the skins were flung into the water
the girls, free of their cages, scrambled after
them, desperate to find their own skins. The

waters frothed and the human sounds changed into the sounds of yelping. The white skin of the girls changed into dark fur. Within moments the maidens had found their seal skins and the young selkies swam to freedom. They swam out of the hall, out of the palace, home to Sule Skerrie, to bear word to Miranda that they were now free but that Magnus Fin, son of Ragnor, was held captive and would soon be forced to give his eyes to the awful false king.

Every seal maiden swam for freedom – everyone that was, except one. Aquella could not find her seal skin. Hers was the skin the monster had damaged in one of his failed attempts to become human. It now lay in tatters on the palace floor, only useful as a warm blanket for a baby shark.

"Oh dearie me! Aquella," said the monster, pouting, seeing the young maiden frantically searching for her seal skin but not finding it. "Still here? Can't find your seal skin then? Oh, the silly sharks must have damaged it at that last fancy-dress party. Never mind. You know I have a soft spot for you and your singing. When I become human I'll take you with me. Yes, that's what I'll do. It'll be lonely up there on the land all alone. I'll take you with me." The monster flicked out one of its tentacles, whipped the edge around the weeping girl and drew Aquella fiercely up beside him. "Pretty one."

Magnus Fin's stomach fell into his feet. *Aquella?* That was the name he had heard Miranda mention. And this was the girl who had been staring at him while she sang her mournful songs. Magnus wanted to tell the monster to let her go immediately, but it seemed his power had left him. He opened his mouth but no sound came out, and any words that were spoken were immediately swallowed into silence by the heavy water.

The monster king glared at the boy. "Shut up, little human. I've had enough of you. Do you honestly think you can command me? Me? The great king? Heh-heh-heh, what a joke. I thought it was funny having a tiny squirt like you giving orders to a great royal like me. It amused me, but enough's enough. Aquella, get back into your cage. Sharks, lock her up."

And with one quick flick of his razor-sharp tentacles, he threw her back into the cage, where a shark swam menacingly towards her and bit the cage closed.

Chapter Twenty-one

Without the sweet ringing music and the presence of the singing girls, a cold eerie feeling fell over the false king's palace. The stagnant water smelled of fear. If there had been anything good, gentle and beautiful in this massive place it had gone, or most of it had. Aquella grasped the bars of her cage and wept. The killer whales hovered at the doorway of the banqueting hall, hoping for leftovers. The hammerhead sharks lurked in the alcoves where the maidens had been and where now only one remained, crying as though her heart would break.

Hundreds of crabs were now busy scuttling over the enormous table, clearing the food into smaller upturned boat hulls for the sharks to polish off. At a sign, the ravenous sharks came in, biting at leftovers wildly in a feasting frenzy. In seconds the food was gone. Then the crabs swept away the shattered remains of their comrades and, Magnus Fin noticed, they had tears in their eyes as they did so.

"Now then, little two-legged thing, will I cut out your eyes or pluck them out, hmmm? What will it be?" The monster came closer, his one eye pulsating like a geyser about to spout.

Magnus Fin, still seated at the banqueting table, kept a tight grip on his moon-stone, holding

it as though he was simply touching his neck.
Not blinded by fear, Magnus found ideas jumped
into his mind. It was easy to see that the great
ugly monster, for all his riches and power, had no
wisdom.

"My tiny eyes will be pin-pricks in your mighty
head," said Magnus Fin. "People on the land will
laugh at you – to be such a great king with such
tiny little eyes. Take them if you wish. I can easily
make another pair. But it would be wiser to make
your own – big powerful eyes that will suit you."

The king was eager to try anything that might
make him human. If this was his chance, then he
had to take it. He had never met a human before,
but despite his size, this little creature seemed
very wise. No one had ever stood up to him like
this before. And if this human teacher said self-
made eyes would suit him better, then self-made
eyes it would be. Yes, he – the great king of the
sea, and soon, the land – would make the most
beautiful and powerful eyes ever known.

"Great idea, little human," the monster said,
nodding his slimy head and shaking his crown.
"You are right, of course. Your tiny little eyes
would not look right on such a magnificent large
head as my own. And I don't want people to
laugh at me!"

Magnus Fin went on, encouraged that the
monster had considered his suggestion and seemed
to have discarded the idea of plucking out his own
eyes. He wracked his brains, trying desperately to
think of a way to outwit the false king. At last he
came up with a plan that might just work.

"Yes, it's easy to make them," he said, "and with all the servants you have, they'll be made in no time."

The monster nodded. He, the great king, did not want to look stupid. He didn't want humans to laugh at him. Yes, he would have two magnificent eyes made: one green and one brown, just like this wise boy's. Green for dominance over the sea and brown for dominance over the land.

"Now listen carefully," said Magnus Fin. "You'll need to brew up dark sand from the bottom of the ocean then mix in some rust from the hull of a sunken tanker. Find petrol and a few batteries. Mix everything into a fine paste and shape it into a circle – as big as you want. That's for your brown eye. For the green eye you'll need to boil up ripe seaweed shoots then find an old green bottle and smash that up. Find a few drops of diesel, mix everything together and you'll have one beautiful green eye. Now for the blue pupils – find traces of mercury. On my way here I saw some dumped first-aid kits. Find a thermometer, break one and capture the mercury, then add it to the crushed shell of a blue periwinkle. Take one tear from a selkie, and shape this mixture into small circles."

No sooner had Magnus Fin uttered his recipe than the monster bellowed out orders for two eyes to be made – immediately: one from brewed dark sand and rust, petrol and batteries; one from seaweed, diesel and smashed green glass; the pupils from shell, one selkie tear and mercury. Instantly the army, the police force, the doctors, the surgeons, the bodyguards, all heeded his order.

Every creature for miles around worked for the king. No matter how ludicrous the command, they were under pain of death to carry it out.

And so thousands of servants set off in search of sand to brew, rust to scrape, mercury to find, green glass to smash, fresh seaweed to pick, winkles to smash, and a tear to stir it all together with.

"I must be the one to gather the tear," shouted Magnus Fin. Desperately he tried to think of ways he could help Aquella. Like his father, she had no seal skin and was trapped in her human form. "The sharks must open her cage; I must mix the eye paste with her tears."

"Open, shut, open, shut, you're making me dizzy! Sharks, open the cage!"

"But your most gracious—"

"Shut up – don't start. And don't contradict me, OK? I know I said shut it two seconds ago but now I'm saying open it, OK?" The monster bellowed, but not as angrily as before. Magnus Fin could tell there was some kind of trembling monster excitement under that thundering bossy voice.

The cage swung open and Magnus Fin swam into the alcove. He cupped his hands together, held them under Aquella's face and gathered her tear.

"I am with you," she said, before Magnus Fin swam back to the table. Magnus felt strength and courage fill him, just knowing there was one other creature in this terrible place on his side. His heart sank hearing the crunching sound of the shark's jaw locking Aquella's cage behind him.

Chapter Twenty-two

Magnus Fin returned to the grand table with Aquella's tear. The servant fish were already back, laden down with broken glass, batteries, seaweed and rust. The banqueting table that once upon a time had been a cruise ship was now a laboratory. Strong great white sharks pulped the ingredients with their teeth then jellyfish stirred the mixture in metal pots. Magnus Fin dropped Aquella's tear into the mercury. Soon the laboratory would be an operating table. Whilst all the hustle and eye-making bustle was going on, the monster drew his tentacles under him and sat on them, leaning his head on the table and staring petulantly at Magnus Fin.

"It's no fun being king any more," he said, pouting. "The sea is dying. I locked Neptune up. I mean, we can't have two great kings, can we? I tried to kill him. Yes, I did. But it didn't work. So I put him to sleep, didn't I. How? Are you asking me how, little human boy?"

Magnus Fin wasn't aware of asking the monster anything, but it was true, the thought clamoured in his head, *how*? How did this stupid, cruel monster manage to overcome the great King Neptune?

"It's great what comes down your human waste pipes." The monster leant closer, as though sharing a secret. "Heh-heh. Little pills, little potions. All sorts of magical things. Easy peasy to put these wonderful little things into Neptune's cavern and kill his water. But there's a little problem, you see: Neptune knows the secret of the waves and he wouldn't tell me, would he. So the sea is dying and I'm bored. It's no fun down here any more. There's no one to talk to around here. I like you, boy; you understand me."

Magnus Fin shrank back, out of flicking range of the vile green tongue. The wide mouth gaped open like a cave. For a second Magnus Fin thought of his father and his cave on the beach, and of his own Neptune's Cave, and he longed to be back home.

"When my new eyes are ready you can take me to the land. I had decided to leave you down here and let you be king, but now I'm thinking it will be good, at first, to have a friend, someone who can introduce me to important people up there. I mean, Aquella doesn't know anybody, does she? What good will she be? You are real. I need someone who can take me to the king and president and prime minister and celebrities. I'll make you my second in command. And I'll need a car. I have seen pictures of how you people get around up there. I won't need legs, just a very big car. A stretch limo."

Magnus Fin was about to tell the monster he didn't own a car, and where he lived they didn't have a king but a queen, when suddenly there was a great commotion at the other end of the table. A fanfare sounded. A conch shell blasted. The eyes, it seemed, were ready. Swimming the length of the great table came two skates and balanced on their

tray-like bodies – the king's new eyes! One round
disk was a dark brown, the other a deep green.
At the centre of each iris lay a circle of deep blue.
Magnus Fin, who had made up the eye recipes
on the spot, was impressed with the servants'
creations. So was the monster.

"Place my beautiful new eyes over my one eye,
side by side, just like the boy's," he bellowed, lifting
his head and lowering it on to the banqueting table
as though it was an operating table. At a sign from
the sharks, the surgeonfish entered. They had been
summoned from warmer waters to undertake this
operation. Carefully they lifted the brown eye off
the skate's back then, with their sharp scalpels,
they placed it down over half of the red eye. Their
scalpels worked quickly, flashing through the water
as they cut into the monster's eye, sewing the plate
of brewed sand, rust, petrol and mercury upon it.

Magnus Fin recoiled at the gory sight. He wanted
to escape. This would have been an opportunity but
Aquella was still locked behind bars. He couldn't
leave her, so he squirmed out of his seat and waded
quickly into the shadows.

The monster groaned and screamed but was
determined to bear it. The surgeonfish now
worked on the second eye, cutting and stitching
and gouging bits out to make space for the new
green eye.

The sight of this operation made Magnus feel
sick. No one saw him wade over to Aquella's cage.
Everyone was focused on the macabre business
that was taking place on the banqueting table. The
monster groaned on.

At last the new eyes were fitted. The eels mopped up the buckets of blood oozing from the old cut and half-gouged-out red eye.

"Finished your maje—" said the chief amongst the surgeonfish. But his words were cut short as the terrible tentacles of the monster lashed round and killed him. The eels left off the cleaning and dabbing, and swam hurriedly away.

"I – can't – see!" roared the monster in agony. "You've blinded me – you – fools! Idiots! Come back and be executed!" But the surgeons that were still alive were now swimming for freedom, beyond the prison-palace gates and back to the warmer waters of the south. Some of the sharks, seeing the king's rising fury and thrashing tentacles, also fled. The monster roared and writhed on the table, throwing his head from side to side, making even more blood spurt from his two new eyes. His crown fell off. Poison from the mercury flooded his brain, the glass and rust cut into him, the battery fluid seeped into his skull.

Aquella's tear seeped down into his monster heart and every creature he had ever killed came back to haunt him. All the pain he had ever caused seared through him now. He screamed. Pain and agony like a thousand burning knives slashed through him. With Aquella's cleansing tear washing him, his evil heart broke.

"It – hasn't – worked … boy," he whimpered. "Help – me!" The few remaining whales, lobsters, sharks and crabs still in the palace took their chance to escape. Only his personal bodyguard the great white shark stayed, but only because he hoped to be king and inherit the palace and all its stolen riches. The great golden gates of the palace were pushed open by a pod of Minke whales, and the monster's tens of thousands of servants fled to freedom. The great white shark took his opportunity and swam fast to the chamber of the locked treasure chest.

In the great hall, the dying monster, a few faithful crabs, Aquella and Magnus Fin remained. The monster screamed and writhed on the table, lashing out with his tentacles. The walls of the palace shook. He thrust his massive tentacles out with such force that the walls began to crumble. Stone by stone, jewel by jewel, plastic bottle by plastic bottle, the whole edifice came loose and tumbled to the palace floor. And the more the monster lashed out in agony, the more jewels and rubbish worked loose. The great palace under the sea fell.

The water turned dark red. Rocks tumbled in slow motion, thundering on to the ocean floor, dislodging sand and skeletons. Magnus Fin was now crouched by the alcove in the shadows, watching the horrific scene. Aquella dived over to her cousin, stretched her arms through the bars and pulled him aside, just before a great cube of gold hurtled down that would surely have crushed him to death.

Rubies the size of rocks crashed down through the dark water, along with old cookers, plastic bags and tin cans. The monster's great treasure chest had been smashed and with it, it seemed, the great white shark. His body slumped down to the seabed and burst apart. Magnus Fin looked down and saw

a tiny crab scuttle across the shaking floor. It took
hold of something small that had burst out of the
body of the shark. Holding this thing between its
pincers, the crab scuttled back to where Magnus
Fin crouched.

"Go," said the crab, "waken Neptune. This is the
key." The brave creature threw the bone up so it
floated through the water and landed in Magnus
Fin's outstretched palm. At that same moment an
almighty groan erupted. Writhing tentacles cut
through the water, dislodging a huge bar of gold,
which hurtled against the cage and set Aquella free.

With that, into the depths of the crumbling
palace, the tiny crab scuttled off. Aquella swam
through the red and black water towards her
cousin. Magnus Fin, with the bone key in his hand,
and now with Aquella by his side, swam hurriedly
across the quaking floor. As they swam the high-
pitched screams of the monster and the roaring
sounds of crashing walls almost deafened them.
Frantically, they waded through the thick murky
water as gold, rubies and rubbish floated down
around them. Deftly Aquella steered Magnus Fin
through the falling treasures. If the water was dim
before, it was utterly dark now, filled with dust
and decay, falling stone and blood.

Magnus Fin and Aquella made it to the gates
just as the whole glittering palace crashed in on
itself, in a watery, slow and awful motion. The
tumbling palace, with all its vast rooms, landed on
the monster. One sickening scream reached their
ears. The dying monster yelled, gasped, whimpered
and was silenced for ever.

Magnus Fin beamed his torch-light eyes through the rubble and blood that filled the sea around him. "I can't see the crab," he cried desperately. "I didn't even thank him." He didn't know if the crab that had given him the precious key had made it out alive or not.

"Come quickly," came an urgent voice.

Magnus Fin turned, and through the dark, murky and churning waters he made out the form of his grandmother, Miranda.

"No! No, I can't leave. The crab that gave me the key, he's still in there." Magnus looked back in horror at the slow crashing rolling gold. Where was the brave crab?

"But, Fin, we must go. You have the key again. Quick! There's no time to lose," said the seal woman, taking him by the hand.

"You have to go," urged Aquella. "You must use the key to waken Neptune. There is no time to lose. I'll find the crab. Go now. Quick." And while Magnus Fin turned towards his grandmother for an instant, Aquella slipped away and swam back towards the fallen palace. She could swim much faster than Magnus and was able to squirm through the smallest of spaces. With her strong hands she pulled aside chunks of gold and rubies, just enough to make a tiny slit in the wreckage, then in a second she was through it. As she entered the devastated place that had been her prison, a huge mound of rubble crashed down.

Magnus Fin glanced back and screamed, "Aquella!"

Miranda scooped the boy into her arms and swam swiftly away through the dark, troubled waters. A thousand sharks, whales, lobsters, crabs, eels and skates swam and scuttled away with them.

"Don't worry, Fin," said Miranda, in her human form and holding Fin now by the hand. "The crab who retrieved the key will find his freedom and Aquella will find hers. We must trust her. Dear Fin, you've been so brave, but it's not over yet. You freed the selkies; you faced the monster and overcame him. Neptune still sleeps and if we don't wake him up soon, the blood of the monster will pollute our beautiful seas for ever. Quick. Don't look back, Fin. In human form, with your help, I hope to withstand the great sleep. There is no time to waste. Son of Ragnor, you must waken King Neptune."

On and on they travelled. Bull sharks guided them. Minke whales, free at last, sang their deep song for them. Magnus Fin's eleven-year-old heart churned inside his chest. The monster was dead, the selkies were free, all except one – and wasn't she the very one who had risked her life for his sake before? Speeding through the water, images flitted through his brain, like a fast-forward film. He saw his father in the cave, his mother in bed, Tarkin in class telling them all about his mermaid, the hideous thrashing tentacles of the monster, draped with plastic and fridges. And then he thought of a green glass bottle he had thrown into the water. Throwing that bottle, he had longed for a new life, friends, adventure. Was he now speeding through water on his way to wake King Neptune because of that bottle?

Still they swam on, and for a long while the thunderous crashing of the monster's falling palace reverberated through the water. Miranda held fast to her grandson while he held fast, with one hand, to his moon-stone, and with the other, to the bone the brave crab had given him. Magnus Fin peered at the strange object with his blue eye-light. It was, he saw with some disappointment, nothing more than a thin white bone – the same he had held once before. He had failed to open the rock door then. Would he fail again? But the brave crab had risked his life for this bone and Aquella had risked her life for the crab. Magnus Fin tightened his grip around it.

"Hurry, Fin," he heard Miranda say, guiding him through the waters. "Use your webbed feet, my grandson. I am tiring; we must be approaching Neptune's cavern. Help me. Don't daydream, Fin. Swim with me. I can't pull you any more, and we're nearly there."

Though the waters they journeyed through were still stagnant and dull, and the waves had long since ceased to flow, there was now a mood of excitement and anticipation in the sea. "We are coming," called Miranda as they glided on over the ribbed ocean floor.

Magnus Fin kicked back the water with his feet and was soon swimming quicker than Miranda. Bending close to her grandson she murmured, "The time has come, son of Ragnor, for the waves to flow again!"

But Magnus Fin could only think of the beautiful and brave Aquella, who had sacrificed herself for him, not once, but twice. And where on earth, or in the sea, was she now? With a heavy heart he swam to King Neptune's palace.

Chapter Twenty-three

"We are close now," said Miranda, slowing down. They had come into a huge kelp forest where fronds of seaweed in shades of purple, green, brown and yellow swayed slowly. Everything was silent. No longer could they hear the echoes of crashing stone, or smell the monster's blood.

Miranda sat for a moment on a mossy rock. Magnus Fin glanced into her eyes and saw the weariness crumple her face again. "Beyond this forest is Neptune's cavern," Miranda said, her voice hushed. "You came here before. Do you remember, Fin?" But Magnus could only vaguely remember; it all seemed such a long time ago, and he had felt tired then, so tired.

"It is dangerous for me to swim beyond our Emerald Valley; see how I have aged, Fin? And if the waves don't return soon I shall die."

Magnus Fin's face darkened with worry. He knew too well about the affliction of sudden age. But Miranda smiled at her grandson and stroked his head. "But have faith, Magnus Fin. You bring strength from the land. See how badly the false king wanted this human power? Remember, Fin – you are living between the worlds – you are born of sea and land. You can open the door."

Magnus Fin felt strong. The bone key no longer felt heavy. His grandmother's words soothed him. "It is the life of the sea I care for – the future sea life, the future fish life, the home of the selkies, Sule Skerrie, and the children that will paddle and swim in this water in the future. I had to allow you to meet the darkness of the sea alone. I left you and you passed the test. Thanks to you, Fin, the monster has been defeated. Had he ruled for much longer the sea would surely have died."

The seaweed forest danced, or so it seemed. Magnus Fin looked into Miranda's eyes. Her words filled him with an urge to do the right thing. As Magnus's strength and resolve grew, Miranda seemed likewise to strengthen.

"Now I can help you," she said, her voice light and filled with excitement. "Quick. Let us go."

Miranda floated upwards, pushing aside the heavy fronds. Revived and her beauty returned, she took Magnus Fin by the hand. "We need to be strong now, Fin, to resist the great sleep." Looking deeply into his eyes she said, "Whatever you do now, Fin, stay awake and keep hold of my hand, and that will keep me strong. This is King Neptune's cavern."

As they glided towards the great rock door beyond the forest, Magnus Fin saw again every glittering shell and waving coral. On either side of the rock, adorned on the great cavernous walls, he could see carvings: fine sculptures of mermaids, fish, seahorses, whales, crabs, seals. He hadn't seen these before.

"Look, Miranda," he called out, "they're beautiful." But his grandmother had no time to look. She was swimming to the tiny keyhole in the great rock.

"Perhaps another time we will be in peace to look," Miranda said, a strain of anxiety in her voice. "There is so little time, son of Ragnor. If we don't waken Neptune soon the monster's blood will poison the whole sea."

Magnus Fin joined his grandmother at the rock and lifted his bone key to the tiny keyhole.

"Quickly, Fin – open the door."

Magnus Fin was determined to succeed, even though this was the very place where he had fallen asleep and where the great white shark had found him. Recalling the sharp pain as the shark's tail grabbed his legs, the boy shuddered. But the shark was gone. The monster was gone. The monster's palace was gone. Magnus Fin wondered that he wasn't grown into a man by now, so much time seemed to have passed. Had he been under the sea for years? Miranda woke him from his reveries. Her soft trembling voice floated into Magnus Fin's thoughts.

"You have the key now, son of Ragnor. You have the key in your hand. Open the door." Magnus Fin looked up and saw that this wise woman, with snow-white hair tumbling down her back, was pointing to his right hand. Her eyes were filled with such love. Sometimes she was seal, sometimes she was human, or was it his eyes that saw her that way? He followed her gaze and looked down to where his hand was clenched around the bone.

"Open it, Fin," she said again. "Open the door."

Magnus Fin stared down at the glistening white bone. His head nodded. His eyes felt so heavy, his limbs like lead. Now, more than anything, he wanted to sleep, sleep for a very long time.

"Open the door, son of Ragnor. Stay awake! Open it. If you fall asleep now, Fin, it's all over."

Her voice jolted him back. He opened his eyes. It was Miranda. She was shaking him. Yes, the bone, the key. Magnus Fin clutched the stone around his neck and instantly woke up. The drowsy sleep fled from him and in a flash he knew what he had to do. He placed the bone into the keyhole and easily, silently, the mighty rock opened. It reminded Magnus Fin of another door, where the handle had been a half-moon of shells. Now the boy stared as the door gave in to a vast circular hallway – like the inside of a whelk – only a million times bigger.

"Come," said Miranda, pulling Magnus Fin by the hand and dodging the sleeping sentry whales at the door, "we must find Neptune." Swiftly they swam through the great cavern. Magnus gazed in wonder as they passed shoals of fish, motionless in the water, not dead but sleeping. They passed mother seals and baby seals lying on rocks, all sleeping. They passed lobsters, crabs, jellyfish, octopus, even mermaids, all fast asleep. Magnus Fin couldn't believe his eyes! There in front of him was a mermaid, with a blue and green shining tail and a garland of shells around her neck, lying on the ocean floor – asleep! Suddenly he thought of Tarkin. The image of his friend made him feel happy.

A deep silence pervaded every cavern, every chamber. Not one creature was aware of the seal woman and the boy who now swam past them. Through many cavernous chambers they swam, walls bright with mother-of-pearl, Venus shells and sea anemones.

Finally they came to a cavern lined with emerald and jade. Half hidden amongst fronds of seaweed and tangles of dulse lay a huge bed made from golden cowrie shells. The mattress was made from sea sponges and the blankets from soft braided sea grass.

Miranda and Magnus Fin had come finally to Neptune's chamber, deep under the sea.

Chapter Twenty-four

On the mighty bed lay the great King Neptune himself, half hidden in masses of seaweed. With every gentle sway of the sea, the fronds of seaweed covered then uncovered his face, itself almost covered with a thick green beard. His long hair swished from side to side. For a moment Miranda's snow-white hair twined into the long green hair of Neptune, like tartan. Apart from the smallest rise and fall in his great chest, the mighty king of the sea looked dead.

Miranda and Magnus Fin gazed down at the sleeping king. Tears coursed down Miranda's face. "Touch his hand," she murmured, "here."

Magnus Fin floated over the great bed and swam to where Miranda gestured. The huge green hands of Neptune lay slumped across his chest. Gently Miranda lifted Neptune's left hand and Magnus Fin held it. The boy's hand was lost in the great palm of Neptune. Barnacles clung to the king's fingernails. Gently Magnus Fin shook Neptune's hand, and as he did Miranda swam up to the true king's sleeping face, whispered, "*Manannán*," and kissed him.

At first there was a stirring, then a shivering, a shuddering then a stretching. Slowly, so slowly, Neptune's lips formed into a smile and, as though waking from a night's deep slumber, the king breathed deeply and yawned.

His eyelashes stirred. Slowly one eye opened, then the other. He yawned again, louder this time, until the great bed shook.

King Neptune had woken up.

And as he did so, every other creature in his palace woke up too. The still silence of moments earlier was gone. Now the great palace rang with movement, yelping, calling, flapping, tumbling, swimming. The creatures awoke, imagining they had been asleep for a few hours, little guessing they had been slumbering eight long years.

For all this time, King Neptune kept hold of Magnus Fin's hand. So huge was the king's hand, Magnus Fin could have sat in it.

"How long has it been, Miranda?" King Neptune spoke. "I believe I have been asleep for a very long time." His voice sounded deep and good. Magnus Fin wanted to rest in the soothing tones of that voice for ever. The boy felt great warmth seep into him.

"Eight years and six days, my good king," Miranda answered. She stroked his mighty cheek and Magnus Fin, as he looked across at his grandmother, saw all traces of her earlier weariness and sorrow drop away. She looked radiant and young.

"The false king?" Neptune asked, his voice veiled now with sorrow at the mention of the evil monster.

"Gone, my lord."

"And the boy? This must be the son of Ragnor? He broke through the threshold then? He found the gap between the worlds?"

"Yes, my lord, this is Magnus Fin, son of Ragnor. He has the gift of both worlds and the time was right. It was he, my great king, who defeated the monster."

King Neptune turned his great head to look now at Magnus Fin. For a moment their eyes met. Gazing into the king's emerald shining eyes, Magnus Fin imagined he saw his father there, then his mother, then Miranda, then Tarkin, then Aquella, then himself. For a split second the green flash of light, the same that had burst out when Magnus Fin had opened the door at the black rock, filled the space between them. A feeling of joy erupted inside him.

"Very few make it over the threshold, young Fin," said King Neptune, "because so many have forgotten the four secrets. Remember them, Magnus Fin: beauty, truth, love and freedom. Take these cowries – to remember."

And into Fin's palm the mighty King Neptune placed four tiny rainbow-coloured shells. Though Neptune was a giant compared with Fin, the tapered ends of his long green fingers were slender. Fin clasped the shells in his hand as Neptune carried on talking.

"Once in a while a child is born who knows the world above and the world below. You are that child, Magnus Fin, and may it not be a great burden to you."

Then he released the boy's hand and rose up from his eight-year bed. "It is time," said the king of the sea, shaking back his hair then turning and swimming out of his chamber. His hair tumbled down his back like seaweed. As he swam he churned the waters to a froth.

Miranda gathered Magnus Fin into her arms and they followed in Neptune's wake. As King Neptune stormed through his palace, every waking creature he passed fell in behind him. By the time he had reached the great cavern rock, a grand procession of sea creatures was awake and ready to bring back the waves.

Neptune ceased his mighty thrashing. He looked at the bone in the lock. "Who found the bone of the Salmon of Knowledge?" he asked. In an instant Miranda was at his side, with Magnus Fin beside her.

"I kept it safe these eight years, my lord," she answered. "Then Magnus Fin, with the help of a brave crab, became the key holder. Magnus Fin opened the door, great king. The same who helped wake you. The same whose father, my son Ragnor, went ashore and married a human. This is the son of the woman who burnt the seal skin and stopped the three-year celebrations."

King Neptune turned for a second time to look at this small boy, dressed in a strange rubber suit, with a moon-stone around his neck. "I thank you," he said.

But before he could say more, Magnus had swum up to the great king's ear and called into it, "My mother says sorry. She wants to be forgiven. Please, King Neptune."

Neptune looked into the boy's eyes. "The eye of the earth is also kind," he said gently, then touched Magnus Fin's moon-stone. "She is forgiven."

In that moment Magnus wanted to go home. He wanted to see his parents. He wanted to see his treasures. He wanted to tell Tarkin all about his adventures under the sea.

"Now return him, Miranda," said Neptune, "before I bring back the mighty waves. We must clean the bad blood. We must wash the waves. See that every ship reaches harbour – that every swimmer reaches land. The dying sea is coming alive."

Miranda pulled Magnus Fin close to her. For a few moments more the boy looked upon the mighty King Neptune, king of the sea. Though he was ready to return home, part of him wanted to stay by King Neptune's side. Part of him wanted never to leave this place, this deep watery world. Salty tears coursed down his cheeks.

As Miranda pulled Magnus away from the door – the very door he had opened – he thought of the crab. Had he been crushed, or had he scuttled to safety? And what of the beautiful Aquella? Where was she? Thinking these thoughts and a hundred others, Magnus Fin was nudged away from the great cavern by the soft nose of his grandmother. Miranda, now in the body of a seal, swam fast, propelling her grandson up and up. Magnus Fin could see rays of sunlight streaming down through the water. He felt the sea turn warmer. They were heading back to the land.

"But what about my hansels?" asked Magnus Fin. He couldn't help wondering about the blessings and gifts he'd been promised, especially the sign from the *Titanic*.

Miranda kept swimming. There was a great urgency now to return her grandson to the land. "You have earned them all, Fin. Some things are given, like talents. Some that are not given have to be earned. You have earned courage, dear Fin. You have learnt to be brave and yes, I have even more hansels for you. But there is no time to lose, Fin. I must return you to the land."

As they swam on, Magnus Fin knew this was true. He had changed in so many ways and gained great riches. He could feel courage pumping through his blood. He felt compassion for Aquella and for the crab, even for the evil monster. At the mention of the word "home" he thought of his father, who he had last seen standing sadly in the kitchen, and he thought of his father's cave, with the wood smoke drifting out and over the sea. He thought of his mother, who he had laughingly called his G-G-P. How was she? And Tarkin – had he chanted? Sometimes under the water he had felt Tarkin with him. *Perhaps friends give you courage*, he thought. Had Tarkin moved back to America? He hoped not.

Magnus Fin imagined he had been under the water for a very long time – perhaps he too would be old when he reached the land. He thought of the treasures in his own Neptune's Cave. Would they still be there?

"The next time you visit us these murky waters will be sparkling clean." Miranda was talking to him. So he could return one day? His dear grandmother was inviting her grandson to return to the sea. Now shafts of sunlight stroked them as they swam upwards. Magnus Fin turned his face to the surface, which shimmered like a ruby glass above him.

"We are nearly there," said Miranda, slowing down. "Tell my son I love him, and tell my daughter-in-law I love her also – and tell them I am so proud of my grandson."

Magnus Fin's face broke into a smile. "I have your bottle, Fin. The bottle you flung into the sea, your wish bottle. None of this would have happened without you wanting it to. I promise you I'll take good care of your wishes. Keep wishing, Fin, never stop wishing."

"But what about my sign from the *Titanic*?" said Magnus because that was the hansel he wanted most of all.

"Ah, patience, Fin."

By now red sunrays streamed down through the water. Miranda rested by a rock – the black rock by the beach. Parting strands of seaweed, she nuzzled her face against it. Magnus Fin's eyes fell upon a cluster of shells in the shape of a crescent moon. It was the handle.

"We have come to the door that will lead you up to the world of earth and air," said Miranda. Magnus Fin felt his head spin, his eyes grow heavy. The seal was letting him go. "I have ships to guide to safety," she said, bending to kiss the boy on the cheek. "Let your father wear the moon-stone for three days and three nights, then let your mother wear it for the same, then you take it back, Fin. Neptune has touched it. And remember – we selkies will always be a part of you. Goodbye, Magnus Fin, son of Ragnor and Barbara."

And pushing open the door, Miranda disappeared. Or was it Magnus Fin who disappeared?

Chapter Twenty-five

Magnus Fin clutched at the jagged black rock. Hoisting himself up through the water, his feet scrambled to find a foothold. Breaking through to the air, he hauled himself upright and breathed. It was low tide. Limpets clung to the sides of the rocks. A shoal of small black fish, disturbed by the sudden splash of a boy in a wetsuit, turned for a moment to stare at Magnus Fin then swam away. A strange feeling came over him, as though he had just awoken from a long and wonderful dream. One of those dreams where you wake up and know that everything has changed for the better. Magnus felt something prick his toe. He looked down and a tiny pink crab with missing pincers travelled over his foot. It scuttled off and disappeared.

Magnus Fin gazed over the skerries towards the beach. Smoke drifted over the water. The smoke was coming from the cave, his father's cave. And there on the beach stood not his father, but Tarkin. He was waving madly and running towards Magnus, splashing through the water, then leaping from rock to rock. The tide was out and the light of the moon plus the light of the setting sun bathed the whole shore in a red glow.

"You did it, Fin, you did it! You were away for three whole minutes," he shouted, excitedly waving his hands.

Magnus Fin jumped from rock to rock towards his friend. With every rock closer to the shore, the world under the sea faded like a dream.

"Hi-fives!" shouted Tarkin, drawing face to face with his friend. The two boys slapped hands together then raced along the beach, and in moments the whole adventure under the sea faded in the mind of Magnus Fin.

When they reached the door of the cottage, the two boys stopped running and leant against the wall, panting like dogs. "I think I beat you, Fin. We were neck and neck but I think I got here first. It's just cos I've got longer legs. And you've got bare feet!"

"OK, you win," said Magnus, gasping. "You're taller. If it was a swimming competition I bet I'd win."

"Yeah, I know that, Fin. You are one cool swimmer. Look, don't tell people at school about me not swimming, OK? Let's keep it secret, and I was thinking, maybe you could teach me. And I could teach you to play guitar. Deal?"

"Yeah," said Magnus Fin, still out of breath and not sure what was real and what was not.

"Cool, I mean, how about we go to Neptune's Cave and you tell me all about it. Like, what was it like under the sea? Did you meet the mermaid?" Tarkin's eyes were gleaming and he tugged at Fin's elbow. "Come on, let's go!"

It came back to Magnus Fin in flashes: being under the water, blood and seals and crumbling stone. It was too soon to talk about it …

Magnus Fin looked at his friend and as he did so more images of his adventure came flooding back. It was real. It had happened.

"Tarkin – I did it. It worked."

"I want to hear all about it. Everything."

They sat on the stone wall outside Magnus Fin's house and he turned the moon-stone round and round in his hands. "It really worked. I went under. I found the door. I met the selkies. I really did go under the sea."

"I know, Fin. I know. I sneaked out of my house. I wanted to be there for you. I saw a flash of green light. I saw the rock open. I was there at the cave. I got there early and made a fire. I wanted to help you, Fin. I chanted a Native American prayer the whole time you were away."

"I thought you said it was just a few minutes?"

"It was."

"But look, Tarkin – I got gifts. You won't believe this but they are from Neptune. I can't remember what they're for though. But cool shells, eh? You can have one." And Magnus Fin stretched out his fist and uncurled it. The four rainbow shells lay in the palm of his hand.

Tarkin stared at the shells as though they were diamonds. "Wow! Oh wow! Can I really, Fin?"

"Yeah – really."

Tarkin looked at each one then finally chose the smallest shell, which was bright green with tiny red dots over it.

Just then someone called out. The boys glanced up and saw the figure of a man running along the beach path towards the cottage. "Hey! Tarkin!" the man shouted at the top of his voice.

"Oh drat, it's Mom's boyfriend!" Tarkin said, jumping off the wall.

Magnus Fin thought of his parents inside. He had already caught a glance of his father peering through the curtain. He would be anxious to know what had happened. And now, of all times, it seemed they had visitors! Tarkin's mum's boyfriend arrived at the garden wall, puffing and panting.

"Tarkin! We were so worried about you! Your mom's in a panic. Where have you been, boy? You should have told us you were going out. Thank God you're OK." He stopped and turned to Magnus Fin. "So this is Magnus Fin? Heard a lot about you and your treasure-hunting, Fin. Tarkin can't seem to talk about anything else," the man said, stretching out his hand to shake the hand of the surprised boy in front of him. Magnus Fin wasn't in the habit of shaking hands and didn't like it much, having his hand pumped vigorously up and down. Suddenly the man let go of his hand and swung round again to his girlfriend's son.

"But it's eleven o'clock at night, Tark, and you are eleven years old. You're just a child! You go out, you ask. Your mother, she's been so darned worried about you."

"Yeah, well, it's midsummer. Look at the moon, and the sun, and Fin here had an adventure, something he had to do, and he needed my help. It was important for me to be here. I thought if I asked, you and Mom would say no!"

"Still, Tark, you should have asked her."

"This was important. You don't understand – Fin needed me."

"Yeah – well, not at this hour. You're a long way from home. Anything might happen ..."

"Home? That's a laugh. Where's home?"

The conversation was going on a while and Magnus Fin began to feel awkward. He sensed his father hiding behind the curtains inside the house, anxious to know about Miranda and the seal folk.

"I've got to go," he interrupted shyly, "sorry. See you tomorrow, Tarkin. Goodbye Mr ... um, bye." Magnus Fin turned and ran up the path to the cottage.

"See ya, Fin," Tarkin shouted, "and thanks buddy," he added, waving his fist with the gift shell in his hand.

"Good night then, Magnus Fin," shouted the man.

Magnus Fin turned and looked at them. He felt sorry for Tarkin, who looked like he might burst into tears. He waved at them both then turned, opened the front door of his house and went inside.

"I'm home," he called as he stepped into the cosy living room. He expected everything to be different. He felt as though he had been away for a long time, but looking around, everything was just as he had left it. Even the fire had hardly died down. He could smell hot chocolate.

His father appeared at the kitchen door with a mug in his hands. "Good to see you, son," he said.

Magnus Fin peered into his father's face, half expecting the deep lines in his skin to melt away.

His father looked at him quizzically then said, "I'll take this hot chocolate to your mother and I'll be right back. Or better still – you take it, son. She likes it when you take in her drink."

So Magnus Fin took the drink in to his mother. It was still light in her room and the last rays of the midsummer sun streamed low on to her face. She took the drink and cupped her hands around the mug.

"I thought it was never coming," she said, smiling. Magnus Fin sat on the edge of the bed and watched his mother wrap her hands round the steaming cup of cocoa.

"Neptune said yes," Magnus whispered. Barbara, sipping, nodded, and a slow fat tear ran down her cheek. She turned and smiled at her son.

"You are forgiven. Neptune said yes," Magnus Fin said again. Thinking perhaps his mother hadn't heard, he repeated himself, louder this time, "Neptune said yes."

But Barbara was so choked with tears she couldn't speak. She could only nod her head, tears now running down her lined face, and landing with a splash into her drink.

'Did the door open for you, son?" Ragnor asked after Barbara had fallen asleep and father and son were sitting together by the fire. Excitement burst through his speech and his deep green eyes shone.

Magnus Fin nodded. Yes, it had, hadn't it? There had been many doors, opening.

"And Miranda?" Ragnor went on. "Did you meet Miranda? Was she waiting for you, son?" Again

the boy nodded. Yes, there had been a Miranda. A
Miranda with long white hair and, so he thought,
a belt of amber and a necklace of shells. There had
been a selkie who had spoken to him, who had
given him a message. His grandmother, sometimes
a woman, sometimes a seal: that was Miranda.

"She loves you," said Magnus and he took off the
moon-stone necklace and put it round his father's
neck. "You've to wear this for three days she said,"
Magnus Fin whispered, "then let Mum wear it for
three days." A tear rolled down Ragnor's old lined
face and he lifted a finger to stroke the stone.

"Did you go to Sule Skerrie?"

Magnus Fin nodded.

"And the waves, Fin? Did you manage to bring
them back?"

Magnus Fin could only shrug. Bringing back the
waves was Neptune's job, wasn't it? Speech was
difficult. It was like waking from a vivid dream
and then having to immediately talk about it. It
had been real, Magnus decided, but now, in the
last rays of the midsummer sunlight, in familiar
surroundings, it seemed so strange. Ragnor sighed,
then father and son turned and stared into the
flames of the fire.

Chapter Twenty-six

The next day after school Magnus Fin and Tarkin were in Neptune's Cave doing their homework. "Seventeen times three is?"

Tarkin chewed the end of his pencil, looking thoughtful. "Well, seven times three is – twenty-one and three times ten is thirty."

"And twenty-one plus thirty is … fifty-one!" Magnus Fin scribbled the answer down. "So what is the square root of sixteen?"

"Square root just means divide it by four, I think. I mean, that's how it was in New York. Maybe in Scotland it's different. Or, um, does it mean divide it by itself? Um, maybe I got it wrong!"

Finding it hard to focus on homework, the image of four shells flashed into Magnus Fin's mind and something about beauty and freedom. "Maybe it was all a dream," he said, suddenly forgetting square roots.

"Or time-travel?" said Tarkin.

"Or magic?"

"Or a near death experience because you dunked your head underwater for three whole minutes?"

They both laughed. Magnus Fin jumped up and brought out the three tiny shells that he had left beside his bed the night he returned from the sea. They were patterned in all the colours of the rainbow. "I remember now – beauty, truth, love and freedom. That's what Neptune said."

"Well, Fin, which one do you think I got?" said Tarkin, staring at the beautiful shells. "Can you remember which shell was which?"

"No, Tarkin. It's hard enough for me to remember what it was like under the sea. Sometimes I remember selkies and a monster and horrible blood and eyes and a bottle and a treasure chest – and even a fridge!" Then Magnus Fin's eyes lit up. "You got the freedom shell. I remember now. You got freedom, Tark."

Tarkin brightened up. "Freedom to stay, do you think?"

"Yeah, why not?" said Magnus Fin.

"But don't you want freedom too?" said Tarkin.

"I've got it and I gave it to you – you can have beauty, truth and love as well. We can share them all. Woo! We're rich!" shouted Magnus Fin, getting up and jumping around his room.

"We're rich, we're rich, we're very, very rich, we got no car but thumbs to hitch, we're rich, we're rich, we're very, very rich, got the sea and the sky and we sleep in a ditch," Tarkin sang, joining Magnus Fin in dancing around the room.

"Hey, Tarkin – you should write musicals." Magnus laughed. "That's not bad."

"Yeah, I get it from Mom. Hey, come on, Fin – I want the whole story. Tell me all about it. Did you see the mermaid?" Tarkin nudged Magnus Fin in the ribs.

"Well – yes, but just once, and she was asleep. But I saw lots of selkies, and loads of sunken ships. And the monster – and the crab."

Tarkin loved the crab. He wanted to know all about it – in detail. "Like, was it a hermit crab or a velvet crab? Did it have barnacles all over its shell?"

And Magnus Fin told his story. And when he'd told it once he had to tell it again. And even when the sun sank in the west, the two friends were still talking selkies and mermaids and monsters and sunken ships and crabs.

"Tell me one more time about the crab. I love that crab. That was just so brave what he did. Wow! Do you think we could go under the sea and you could take me with you? I mean, once I've learnt how to swim. Then I'd see the mermaid – and the crab. D'you think so, Fin?"

"Yeah, sure. Miranda said I'd go back. She said I would."

"I'm sure it would be OK if I went with you, Fin. I'm special too. Remember, I saw a mermaid and Dad couldn't see her – or hear her? I did. I can't wait for you to teach me how to swim. When are you going to start the swimming lessons, Fin?" Tarkin asked, shaking his friend's arm. "I'll bring my guitar round. I'll teach you 'Smoke on the Water'. Hey, Fin. You OK? You look funny, man."

Magnus Fin shook himself then laughed. "Yeah. I'm fine. Fine. It's just – you might go away. You said you might."

Tarkin grew silent and twisted the end of his ponytail. "Yeah, but, we could – you know, Fin –

keep in touch." But Tarkin's voice didn't sound as hopeful as he tried to make it.

Magnus Fin forced a smile. "Well, I hope you don't leave." Then he remembered the shells he had been holding all this time in his hand. He lifted them to his ear. "Listen, Tarkin," he gasped, "they're making a noise! I can hear the waves crashing."

Tarkin brought his ear to the cowrie shells and listened. "Wow! Oh, man, that is wild. What a din!"

Then Magnus Fin pressed the shells close to his ear and imagined he could hear the voice of Miranda singing, "Son of Ragnor, the waves are crashing again."

"Come on, Tarkin," called Magnus, jumping to his feet, "race you down to the sea."

Tarkin leapt up and followed Magnus out of the house and along the shore path. The two boys ran like the wind, Magnus Fin's mop of black hair bouncing up and down, Tarkin's long blond ponytail streaming behind him. Panting hard, they stopped before they reached the beach, and their jaws almost fell to their feet. Huge crashing waves twenty feet high reared up then flung themselves, white and thunderous, against the rocks.

"Wow, looks like a roller-coaster ride," shouted Tarkin, wishing he had a surfboard and wishing he could swim. The two boys whooped and yelled. They ran into the sea when the waves sucked back and ran out when the waves pounded in. Salt spray splashed over them. They yelled and got soaked as the waves rolled in, smashing over the rocks and cliff sides, flinging spray far up in the air.

As they watched the mighty waves, everything the sea had swallowed for years was spewed up. Hundreds of plastic bottles were flung on to the beach and then more: car parts, batteries, ropes, nets, tin cans, bicycles, crash helmets, forks, tents, dead sheep, all hurled back to the land. Norwegian milk cartons, Orcadian juice bottles, Swedish washing-up liquid, broken boats, creels, oil drums, bits of toys, all flung themselves at Magnus Fin and Tarkin's feet. The two boys yelled at the top of their lungs when a huge wave soaked both of them.

And as they ran up the beach with the waves crashing and smashing just yards from them, they looked up and saw they weren't the only ones on the beach. Ragnor was coming towards them, waving and walking as fast as he could. The limp, Magnus Fin thought, didn't look as bad as it usually did.

Behind him the boys could see a crowd of people. They were swarming down from the village, some running, and some walking, all eager to see the leaping waves. Mrs McLeod was amongst them. She approached Tarkin and Magnus Fin with a big smile on her face.

"Looks like you boys have got some work to do cleaning this beach," she laughed. "See you on Monday. And Magnus Fin," she said, winking at him, "be on time!"

Chapter Twenty-seven

Magnus Fin was on time that Monday morning. So was Tarkin. All the pupils were excited about going to the beach, especially as Mrs McLeod had promised them all a chocolate bar after the big clean-up. Hardly anyone in the village had been able to sleep for the noise of huge waves thundering and smashing on the shore all night long. They were still crashing and breaking and jumping high like wild white horses when the class left the school. Wearing their wellies and old clothes they all trouped down to the beach.

Only Sandy Alexander didn't turn up. When Patsy asked where he was, Mrs McLeod told her, "Sandy? Scared to even look at the sea after he nearly drowned the other day. Him and his big brother and his dad! It was quite a miracle that one." Magnus Fin overheard and in a flash the image came back to him of dragging a boy up through the water, not just one boy but two. He shook his head in disbelief; so that was Sandy Alexander and his brother?

"Right, P6. It's nearly time for your good deed," the teacher said as they came closer to the beach. "Now when we get there everyone has got to fill at least two bags full of rubbish, all right? Don't, I repeat, don't touch broken glass or anything that looks dirty. Mostly what we're going for is plastic bottles, got that?"

The twenty pupils of North Bay School nodded. "When do we get our chocolate?" asked Patsy Mackay, who had been making funny faces all through Mrs McLeod's speech. She was wearing a new white sparkly top and smart pink wellies with love hearts all over them. She looked as though she'd rather die than pick up rubbish.

"When you've filled two bags," said the teacher, "full! We'll soon be there, children. I can see the rubbish from here."

The whole class had to march right past Magnus Fin's house on their way down to the beach. As they did so, every single pupil turned and peered in through the cottage windows, trying to catch a glimpse of the strange parents they'd heard so much about. They were taken aback when an elderly-looking man came to the door and waved. Magnus Fin grinned and felt, for the first time in a long time, proud.

"That's my dad," he said to his teacher, and he waved back.

Some other children waved too and Tarkin shouted, "Hi, Ragnor! How's it going, man?"

Then they noticed a woman at the window, and she too was waving. "And that's my mum," said Magnus Fin, and his walk took on such a bounce you'd think he was skipping down to the beach.

"Oh! Really," said the teacher, and muttered something under her breath about them not looking too bad – not nearly as bad as she'd imagined.

It was a hard morning's work. Each child, even Patsy Mackay, with her nail polish and hand cream and twenty bangles dangling away on her wrist, easily filled their two bags, and there was still a lot more rubbish strewn the length of the beach.

As Magnus Fin filled his bags, cramming them full of plastic bottles and broken pieces of plastic and rubber, he gazed out to sea. His thoughts forever wandered off to Aquella. He wished he could see her. He wished she was all right.

"Dreaming, Magnus Fin?" It was his teacher, checking up on her pupils. "A penny for them," she said gently.

"Oh! Hello, Miss. I've finished my two bags," he said, shaking himself from his thoughts. "Um, when do we get our chocolate?" Mrs McLeod laughed and gave Magnus his bar of chocolate.

"Any washing baskets in there by any chance?" she added, but Magnus Fin was too busy pulling the wrapper off his chocolate to be thinking about washing baskets.

As soon as Mrs McLeod had gone, Magnus Fin found himself thinking about Aquella again and a heavy feeling pulled at his heart. Even the chocolate he loved didn't taste as good as it usually did. "Wish," Miranda had said, "never stop wishing." So he closed his eyes tight and wished with his whole heart that Aquella was safe and well – and that somehow, somewhere, he would see her again.

Someone else was wishing too. Tarkin had been busily stuffing his bags full of rubbish when he found a beautiful blue glass bottle complete with cork. He looked at it and held it up to the sunlight. It sparkled. It had worked for Magnus Fin, so maybe a message in a bottle would work for him too.

He looked around and saw the other pupils were busy gathering rubbish and the teacher was far off. Quickly Tarkin pulled a pen out of his pocket, the pen he always kept for emergencies. He'd never actually had an emergency before but his dad had always told him, "Have a pen on you, Tarkin – you never know when you might need it."

This was it. Trouble was, he didn't have any paper. Magnus Fin was nearby, staring out to sea and eating a bar of chocolate. The chocolate bar had paper on it. That would do. He dashed over to Magnus, grabbed the paper, saying, "It's an emergency, Fin, I'll explain it all later," then dashed back to his spot on the beach. There wasn't much space on the back of the chocolate wrapper. He'd have to write very small:

Hi whoever u r,
   I'm Tarkin. I wanna stay here. I don't wanna go. And I want Dad to visit. This is the best place ever and Fin's the best friend ever. Please, sea.
   Thank u xx

He folded up the chocolate wrapper and pushed it down into the blue bottle. With the next huge wave that came, he pushed the cork as far down as he could then hurled the wishing bottle out to sea. The wave sucked it up, bobbed it about and in seconds it was far out at sea.

Magnus Fin saw his friend and shouted to him, "Good luck!" But his voice was drowned out by the din of the waves.

Chapter Twenty-eight

Two days later – as Magnus Fin ran up the road to the village, trying desperately not to be late for school – Ragnor had an unexpected visitor. A young girl with long dark hair knocked on the door of the cottage by the sea. She wore a tattered blue dress and was completely drenched to the skin. She had come in search of her uncle Ragnor …

Tarkin turned up at school even later than Magnus that day, looking glum. He hadn't even bothered to tie his hair back and it hung like a damp curtain across his face. He spent the morning chewing on his hair and scratching his name on the desk, TARKIN WAS HERE. At lunchtime he gave his bag of crisps, that he called "chips", to Magnus Fin.

"Mom doesn't like it here any more," he said, kicking a stone across the playground. "It's too cold, she says. And she can't get the right inspiration for writing her musicals. When she starts to go on like that it usually means we'll be packing our bags."

Tarkin's eyes filled up with tears and he kicked another stone, annoyed that his message in a bottle had brought the opposite of what he wanted. "I don't want to go anywhere else. I wish she'd just stop, you know? Like, just live somewhere. You're lucky, Fin. You've never been anywhere else."

"Well, I've been to Inverness a few times and I've been to Aberdeen once and I've been to Glasgow once," he said, counting all the places he had been on his fingers. "And I've been at my granny's in John O'Groats loads of times."

"Yeah, Fin, but you know what I mean. Like, you haven't been dragged across the world looking for the perfect place. The perfect place that just doesn't exist. Your dad wasn't dumped somewhere along the line cos he couldn't keep up. You don't have to get to know people every few months when you turn up at the next random school. You don't have to live out of a suitcase."

"I thought you said you liked the Inuits and the Aborigines?" Magnus Fin said, trying not to think about Tarkin packing a suitcase and going away. It didn't seem fair. Magnus Fin's bottle had brought him a best friend and now it seemed he might be taken away.

"Sure I like them. They stay in one place! They know the land they live on, every blade of grass. Not like me. I'm just getting to know this place. The beach. The cave. The hills around here. The sea. I really like this place, Fin – and you. Not everyone likes me. You don't think I'm weird. You're cool, Fin. Real cool."

Just then the bell rang and the children filed into the classroom. Mrs McLeod called for the class to be quiet. "Right, P6. Good afternoon. I must say how well you have all done. Everyone in the village is saying so and your picture will be in the local paper on Saturday, so well done, children. Yes, the beach clean-up was a great success. Although it looks like we might have to do it again next week."

A cheer ran round the class, except for Patsy who said no way was she going to do that again.

"Anyway, that wasn't what I wanted to say," the teacher continued. "If you'll just quieten down, I have something to announce."

The class grew instantly quiet. Announcements usually meant there would be a school disco or an outing or they'd get away early or an astronaut was coming in to give them a talk.

"Right, very good. Excellent. We have a new pupil joining us. Isn't that nice? I know it's a bit unusual to join when it's nearly the summer holidays but it'll give her a chance to settle in and get to know you all, then she'll be back with you all for P7."

The class was silent. A new girl joining was a big thing. She might be really nice, she might be really horrible, she might be a bully, she might be rich, she might be funny, or she might have a dad with a helicopter. "I'll just bring her in. She's talking to the headmistress right now. See if you can make a very good impression, P6, and be as good as gold when the new girl comes in."

"What's her name, Miss?" asked Chloe Grant, who was upset that there were three Chloe's in the class already and dreaded there being a fourth.

"Don't worry, Chloe Grant," the teacher said, "she is not called Chloe."

"So what is she called? Tell us, Mrs McLeod," chanted Chloe Gunn and Chloe Gow.

"Her name," said the teacher, looking around the room, wondering where the new girl would sit, "is Aquella, and she's Magnus Fin's cousin. Magnus, as there is space, she can sit next to you."

The teacher marched out of the classroom and Magnus Fin sat with his mouth wide open until Tarkin nudged him and told him he looked like a goofy goldfish after brain removal.

Two minutes later Mrs McLeod came back into the room, and this time, tucked in behind her, was the new girl. Magnus Fin hardly dared look up. His heart was pounding under his ribs like there was a football match going on inside him. He counted to ten then raised his head. His eyes fell upon the new girl – his cousin. It was her. It really was. It was Aquella! It was the girl he had met under the sea. He knew it would be.

Ever since flinging his bottle out to sea, magic things had been happening non stop. *Why*, he thought, *should they stop now?* He stared at her and a tingling feeling ran up and down his spine. She, like him, was a selkie. Without all her shell necklaces and skirts of seaweed she looked, of course, different. Anyone else would think she was an ordinary human girl (although Tarkin would later tell him there was no such thing as an ordinary human). Magnus Fin saw how emerald-green and shining her eyes were and how sleek and jet-black was her hair. It was so shiny he could almost see Mrs McLeod's face reflected in it. The new girl was a selkie; that was for sure. She was wearing human clothes and she had tied her long hair back into a ponytail, but there was no mistaking: this new girl was the one he had last seen diving back into the rubble of the dying monster's palace. She looked across at Magnus Fin and smiled.

"Well, P6. Don't be rude. Say hello and welcome to Aquella."

"Hello and welcome, Aquella," they chorused in their sing-song group voice.

Then the new girl sat down next to Magnus Fin. On the other side of Magnus sat Tarkin. Both boys stared at Aquella, who turned and winked at them then sat back and listened to the teacher.

"So, P6. Aquella is rather shy, and who wouldn't be, not knowing anyone, so the headmistress has asked me to say a few words. She comes from a little-known island north of Shetland. Aquella is pronounced *Akwa-ella* – lovely name, don't you all think?"

The pupils craned their necks to get a better look at Aquella. The teacher smiled encouragingly at the new girl and carried on. "I want you all to be kind to our new girl and make her feel at home. We are, are we not, P6, a very friendly class?"

The whole class nodded.

"And Aquella's background may be different from our own, but we are all, are we not, P6, in our different ways, different?"

The whole class nodded.

"And there's nothing wrong with being different, is there, P6? In fact, we should celebrate our differences, don't you all agree?" Mrs McLeod could feel herself getting carried away. Some of her husband's influence was definitely rubbing off on her. She beamed down at the children, suddenly overwhelmed with love for every single one of them – the chubby and the skinny, the grubby and the funny, the fussy and the bossy. Every single one of them. Even that Magnus Fin.

Three heads at the front nodded particularly vigorously: one with long blonde hair, one with long black hair and one with a mop of black hair that used to be short but was now, the teacher noticed, almost touching his shoulders.

"So now, P6, as you've all been so good and so hard-working, and as it will soon be the summer holidays, I think you deserve a story."

They all cheered. "Anyway, P6, as Tarkin, I'm sure you'll all remember, told us such a wonderful story about a mermaid ..." They all cheered again. "... I thought I'd tell you one too. This is one my husband told me, not about a mermaid exactly, but about a creature we have in Scotland. So, children, are you all listening?

"Once upon a time there was a seal ..."

Chapter Twenty-nine

At playtime everyone hovered around Aquella. They wanted to hear how a girl from north of Shetland would talk. Magnus Fin was proud to introduce everyone to his new cousin. He couldn't quite believe that he now had two friends! He couldn't ask her the questions that were burning inside him, not with all the other children milling around. So he had to wait until hometime.

As they wandered towards the cottage by the shore, Aquella told Magnus how Miranda knew Aquella wouldn't survive long in Sule Skerrie without a seal skin; how Miranda had led her up to the rock with the mother-of-pearl handle. Just as Magnus Fin had done, Aquella came ashore.

"Miranda brought me a blue dress she had found in the wardrobe of a sunken ship. She gave me directions to your cottage and told me to ask for my uncle Ragnor. Your mum and dad gave me food and clean clothes – and a room in the attic that looks out to sea."

Magnus Fin could barely contain his excitement. "But, Aquella, what about the monster's ruins – and the crab? Did you save the crab?"

"Ah yes, the brave crab ..." said Aquella and she smiled. Although it wasn't an answer exactly, Magnus Fin felt sure the crab had survived.

Just then they reached the cottage door and an unusually animated Barbara welcomed her son and her new niece inside.

Aquella, Magnus Fin and Tarkin became the best of friends. They were rarely out of each other's sight. Magnus Fin's life was choc-a-bloc busy these days. He could hardly believe that only a month ago he was friendless and not very good at talking to people. Now it seemed he was chatting all the time, and running, and playing, and teaching swimming. Aquella didn't say anything about being a selkie, but sometimes she and Magnus Fin gave each other what Tarkin called "the emerald-flash look" and in that look everything was said. Perhaps, thought Magnus Fin, selkies didn't need words.

Sometimes eleven-year-olds didn't either, and at those times the three friends just played at the seaside or in Magnus Fin's Neptune's Cave without saying anything at all. At other times they chatted about everything under the sea and sun. Aquella enjoyed her life as a girl, especially with friends like Magnus Fin and Tarkin. But Tarkin, Magnus Fin noticed, didn't laugh and joke as much as he used to.

"What's up with you, Tarkin?" he asked him one day.

"Yeah, Tarkin," said Aquella, "you haven't told a joke for ages."

"I get the feeling she really wants to go," he told them, twisting his ponytail round his little finger then biting on his shark's tooth. The three of them were on their way to the village shop to buy sweets. "Mom, she says it's too cold here. She says if this is summer, what's winter gonna be like? She keeps talking about France now. She got a book out of the library about farmhouses in the south of France."

"Maybe she'll change her mind," Aquella said. "The tide changes all the time, doesn't it? So maybe people change their minds too?"

"Yeah, Tarkin, I bet Aquella's right. I think your mum will change her mind. You can't go yet anyway. You haven't learnt to swim yet," said Magnus Fin, nudging his friend in the ribs. "Um, and my mum and dad want to have a party. So, Tarkin, why don't you invite your mum and her boyfriend? Come round on Saturday. Mum will bake you a cake."

Tarkin raised his eyebrows. "Really?" He hadn't seen Magnus Fin's parents for a few days, but he couldn't imagine they would ever organise a party.

"Really," said Magnus Fin. "We'd have no party without Tarkin, isn't that right, Aquella?"

"That's right," she said, smiling, "and this is going to be my very first party. I can't wait!"

Chapter Thirty

That Saturday, the cottage down by the sea was filled with the sweet cinnamon-and-sugar smell of baking. Ragnor was busy trying to coax the barbecue to work, and Barbara was in the garden shaking out a white tablecloth and throwing it over the picnic table.

"Food will be ready soon, everyone," Barbara called out, picking daisies from the grass then scattering them over the tablecloth. Then she turned and ran across the grass to where Ragnor was busy with the business of sausage cooking. He had finally succeeded in getting the coals to light. The two of them laughed, hugged each other then ran hand in hand up to the bench, where they plonked themselves down and, arms round each other, gazed out to sea. Barbara's long red hair fell down her back and spun out as she shook her head and laughed. Ragnor's hair was also long. His was black and shiny. From where Tarkin, Magnus Fin and Aquella were playing swingball, they could hear the rich, warm laughter coming from the two grown-ups.

"So, like, who are these cool people, Fin?" Tarkin asked, nudging in the direction of the handsome man and woman on the bench.

"My parents," said Magnus Fin, his voice bursting with pride.

"Cool," said Tarkin. "So what happened to the G-G-Ps? Where are they? I mean, I thought your parents were, like, ancient?"

"I think they time-travelled," said Magnus Fin, winking and wishing everyone was as positive as Tarkin. "And, um – see that lady doing a spot of line dancing over there in the cowboy boots and big hat? That's my granny!"

Hearing herself mentioned, Granny May turned and waved.

"Cool, Fin, you are unique – totally awesome. Oh man, I wish I wasn't going to France. I can't even speak French. Aquella, that just ain't how you hold the bat. Look, it's like this, that's it."

"I've got a lot to learn," said Aquella, winking at Magnus Fin. Then she turned back to Tarkin who had just whacked the ball really hard. "Hey, Tarkin, where's your mum? I thought she was coming to the party?" Aquella missed the ball. "Oh! Bad shot! Hey, this is my very first party and she isn't even here!"

"I dunno where she is. I wanted to get here early. She said she was going for a walk down the beach then she'd be here. Maybe she's fallen out with her boyfriend."

Just as the sausages were ready, the rest of the children in Magnus Fin's class at school turned up.

"Heard you were having a party," said Patsy Mackay. "Aquella told us."

"I hope that was all right," said Aquella. "We're all friends, aren't we?"

For a second Magnus Fin looked uncomfortable, until Tarkin nudged him.

"Cool," said Tarkin, "means we can play lots of games – like hide 'n' seek. Man, I love hide 'n' seek. Do you, Aquella?"

"Never tried," she said, "but I'm sure I'll love it."

Magnus Fin grinned and Patsy Mackay threw him a big tooth-gap smile, then Ragnor called out at the top of his voice, "Food's ready, everyone!"

While Barbara handed everyone napkins and drinks, the guests could only stare, blink and look on in wonder. Magnus Fin's mother was a picture of beauty. By this time, half the village had turned up. Even Granny May, puffed out after the line dancing, was stuck for words. Eventually, after a bite of sausage, she recovered her speech and with tears in her eyes announced to everyone, "She is even more beautiful than I remember. What did I tell you, Fin? What did I tell you? Everyone – isn't she an absolute beauty? Isn't my daughter just a picture? Thank goodness they're better, that's all I can say."

And not only Magnus Fin, but Ragnor and all the guests could only nod their heads and smile.

"Oh, for heaven's sake, stop staring and eat up," said Barbara, putting her hands to her face, hardly daring to believe that her youth and beauty had returned. "You don't want these sausages to get cold, do you? And then there's chocolate cake and ice cream for afters." Then Barbara turned to Tarkin and saw he wasn't eating his sausage, just fiddling with it. "What's wrong, Tarkin?" she said gently. "Don't American boys like hot dogs?"

"Yeah, usually, it's just …"

"It's just that he might have to go away, Mum," said Magnus Fin, his mouth crammed full of sausage, "cos his mum thinks it's too cold here."

"Where is she anyway?" Ragnor said, coming over to put thirty more sausages on the barbecue seeing as half the village had turned up. "I thought you said she was going to come to our party, Tarkin?"

But Tarkin could only shrug his shoulders and scuff his feet. Words seemed to have left him. He didn't know where she was. Packing a suitcase probably and stabbing a pin into a map of France.

"Isn't that her?" said Aquella, pointing to a woman and man walking down the path towards them.

Tarkin looked up. Yes. It was. He nodded. Then looked again. His mother had something in her hands. As she came closer, Tarkin saw what it was. His bottle! The blue glass bottle he had flung out to sea two weeks before. Of all the people in the world to find it, his mother had! His face flushed red.

"Welcome to the party," said Barbara, walking up to greet the couple. "You're just in time for some of Ragnor's wonderful sausages."

Tarkin's mum smiled at Barbara. "Thank you so much. So good of you to invite us. I just gotta go and talk to my son first if you'll excuse me." And she walked through the crowd of guests to where Tarkin stood at the bottom of the garden, with his head down, staring at the grass. She looked at him and lifted his chin. "Look at me, Tarkin."

"Why?" he said, embarrassed about the message in a bottle. He thought maybe she would give him a row about it. What bad luck. Of all the people in the world to find his bottle.

"Honey," she said with tears now glistening in her eyes, "I found it. The waves brought it in when I was out walking." She held the bottle up for him to see.

Tarkin didn't know what to say. He stared at his mother and swallowed hard. He hoped he wasn't going to burst into tears. There was no doubting it, the bottle she now held in her hands was the bottle he had thrown to sea.

"I didn't know, honey," she said, shaking her head. "I didn't know you found it so hard. I thought maybe you liked all this travelling. I thought we'd find the perfect place one day. I'm sorry, Tark. Will you forgive me?"

Tarkin swallowed again and nodded his head. Still no words came, but he found his embarrassment was gone and suddenly he felt happy that she had found his bottle.

"I'll make a huge effort, Tark. I promise. What does it matter if it's cold? Hm? It is good here. It could be home. We could make it home, son. I'll get me a big fur coat like the one you found in the Yukon – and I'll ask your dad to come and visit you. He'd love to, Tark. I know he wants to."

Then Tarkin did cry. He couldn't help it; too many big things were happening all at once. Then he hugged his mother and told her how much he loved his new friends and his new school, and Scotland, and how he wanted to stay for years and years, and that if she did get a fur coat it should really be fake. He only stepped back when he heard loud cheers coming from Magnus Fin and Aquella and Ragnor and Barbara and Frank and Mrs McLeod and all the other guests.

"Three cheers for Tarkin – he's going to stay – hip-hip-hooray!"

"Magic!" said Tarkin, as happy now as he had been sad just ten minutes earlier. "It really does happen. It happens to me too, Fin. Wow! I'm staying!"

"Magnus Fin! Tarkin! Aquella! Children, hurry, come and look!" Ragnor, Barbara and Tarkin's parents called out and waved everyone over. The children dashed up to where the adults stood, all of them shaking their heads in wonder and staring out to sea.

"Look," said Barbara eagerly, "look, boys, look at these wonderful waves. Aren't they enormous? And there's something flashing out there in the sea. Look – can you see the tail?"

Everyone stared to where Barbara was pointing, to a place beyond the black rock where spray splashed from the rippling sea. For a fleeting moment a cream-coloured glinting tail flicked out of the water and the most beautiful seal breached in an arc.

"Wow!" gasped Tarkin. "That was huge!"

"She's amazing," shouted Magnus Fin, waving wildly as the beautiful creature yelped, dived under the water and was gone. Ragnor laughed at the two gawping boys.

"Hey, boys," he called out, "now don't go falling for a seal."

"And why not?" said Barbara. "The best creatures in the world in my opinion. We can learn a lot from them," she said, squeezing her husband's arm.

Aquella lifted an arm and waved at the creature that dived under the water. Much longer than anyone else, she stared out to sea then wiped a tear from her cheek. She took a very deep breath then turned to her uncle Ragnor. He was standing behind her, waiting for her to say goodbye to the seal.

"It's all right, Aquella," he said, holding her tight. "And you know, it's not too bad being human," he said warmly. "In fact, sometimes being human is the very best thing in the world."

Then Tarkin, Aquella, Magnus Fin and even Patsy Mackay had a big group hug.

Then everyone at the party ate chocolate cake – loads of it, with vanilla ice cream and chocolate sauce.

And the rays of the sun sparkled on the sea.

And the clear blue waves broke white on to the shore.

Magnus Fin had never felt so happy in his life. While everyone was chomping on cake, he ran down to the shore and on to the skerries. The waves crashed over them, white and sparkling. He leapt easily from rock to rock, excited at the booming music the waves made.

Magnus Fin reached the edge of a jutting rock just as an almighty wave crashed over the rocks and soaked him. When the wave withdrew, three things were left on the glistening rock, lying like gifts at Magnus Fin's wet feet: a trainer for his left foot, another for his right and – Magnus Fin gasped – a large, wonderful treasure. He yelled for joy, bent down and picked it up.

CAPTAIN'S QUARTERS

His hansel.

Read on for an intriguing sneak preview of
Magnus Fin's next adventure in

MAGNUS
FIN
AND THE
MOONLIGHT MISSION

Magnus Fin ran along the shore path in the grey dawn light. He cut down to the sandy beach, kicking up tangles of seaweed as he ran. Feeling like the king of the sea and shore, Magnus Fin let out a loud whoop. An oystercatcher down at the water's edge whooped back.

Being alone at the beach in the early morning was always special, but low-tide mornings like this were even better. Low tide meant secret rock pools, each like a miniature ocean. It meant more stones to scramble over. And it meant he'd be able to see the top of the mast of the sunken ship.

In a flash Magnus Fin was down on the skerries: the sloping black rocks that went out to sea. They spent half their lives hidden underwater. Now here they were, craggy, slippery and full of surprises. Fin leapt over stones and slithered on seaweed. He hoisted himself up his favourite rock, the high black one that jutted above all the others. Fin's feet knew its ledges and craggy footholds. Panting hard he reached the top and stood tall, just in time to see the beaming orange sun burst over the sea's horizon. What an entrance! Up and up it rose, like King Midas, turning everything to gold.

Magnus Fin whipped out his penny whistle. He could only play one tune but he played it well and he played it twice. And sure enough, up they came, their sleek round heads lifting out of the shining water. A wide smile burst over the boy's face. Quickly he counted – sixteen, seventeen, eighteen seals – and every one of them watching him. There were black ones, mottled grey ones, small silver calves and huge long-whiskered bulls.

Fin pocketed his whistle, took a deep breath, cupped his hands round his mouth then shouted, "Hello seals!"

He waited for the reply. And it came: shy at first, then lifting into a rousing choir – the seal's song. Yelping, honking, booming, soft for a moment then soaring! Like a trumpet, a bass guitar, a bodhran, bagpipes! What a sound!

When their song ended Magnus Fin clapped loudly, and the seals, lifting their flippers and splashing them together with yelping cries, clapped too. One by one they flipped, kicked their tail fins, then silently dipped under the water and vanished. Behind them the black thin mast of the sunken ship remained, like a finger, pointing to the sky.

By this time the sun was up and the chill of the November dawn was gone. Glancing behind him, Magnus Fin saw that everything was on fire. The golden sand on the beach shone. The hillsides and cliff faces glowed, meaning (because he could read time by the sun) that it was quarter past eight. That gave him half an hour to scramble about on the skerries, study the rock pools, then comb the beach before a quick breakfast, then school.

In his Neptune's cave of a bedroom Magnus Fin had a growing collection of pottery bits. He planned to make a mosaic picture, once he'd found a few more pieces of broken plates and coloured glass. The tide line was the best place to find broken pottery. Blue bits – that's what he wanted.

And that's what he was thinking about when he bent his knees and swung his arms back, ready to jump from the high rock ... when something by his feet caught his eye. He dropped his arms and stared.

To the side of his right foot he saw a strange white mark. Gull droppings? He peered closer. It didn't look like gull droppings. His heart skipped a beat. No one knew that rock like he did. He got down on his knees to examine it.

Goosebumps crept up his arm. The mark looked like writing. But this was his rock, his lookout tower. Being high up, this rock let him see what the black-backed gulls were up to, puffins even if he was lucky, and most importantly, the seals. So what was this mysterious white mark doing on his rock? It hadn't been there the day before, he was sure about that.

Forgetting his plan to search for pottery, Fin stared at what appeared to be silvery writing. He let his finger follow its trail. It looked and felt like the letter M. Fin pulled his finger back and a shiver ran down his spine.

He glanced over his shoulder to the sea. The seals had gone. Normally they stayed close by, tumbling over in the water, or simply staring at him with their large kind eyes. Where were they?

Fin looked over his shoulder and scanned the beach. Not even a dog walker was out this early.

You're brave now, remember that, he said to himself, standing up straight. And it's only a silly mark on the stone. A rusty nail on a piece of driftwood tossed on a high wave could have made that mark.

Magnus Fin looked around for driftwood but, save for a tangle of seaweed and a plastic bottle, nothing else had been brought in by the tide.

He peered out over the bay. It was a crinkly kind of sea and, apart from the swishing sound of the waves breaking over the skerries, it was quiet. Most of the sea birds had flown south for the winter. Only the oystercatchers patrolling the shoreline and a few gulls bobbing on the waves remained. And they couldn't write the letter M on his rock, could they?

He tried to shake off the mood. He bent down and rubbed his hand over the M to erase it, but the harder he rubbed the stronger it became.

"Don't be daft, Fin – it's nothing," he said to himself out loud. Then he said it again, even louder, "Nothing at all!"

Shouting like that made him feel braver. He remembered the way he had bawled out for joy just a short while ago. He tried whooping again but it didn't sound the same, and the oystercatcher didn't bother answering.

Magnus Fin jumped down, landing on a shelf of rock below. Now his heart really did thump wildly. Scrawled upon the ledge of rock, the letter F stared up at him.

M. F.

He bent closer. And gulped. Jeepers creepers, there were more! Loads of tiny scrawled initials. The rock was shouting with Ms and Fs! Fin felt his knees turn to jelly.

Something, or someone, was trying to contact him.